Rescue Mission

Now through the shifting mists, they could glimpse the great multi-colored maw of the Thunder River Canyon and they lifted their mounts to one last, tearing burst of speed. Dex knew where the head of that trail lay; it was marked by the jumble of sandstone outcrops that had hidden it cunningly. He headed for that cluster of broken stone.

Wasatch pealed a shrill warning. Out of those rocks, dead ahead, a figure had reared upright—a dark and towering figure in the dress of one of Alviso's renegades. The fellow had a rifle at his shoulder and, even as Dex glimpsed the weapon, he saw a spike of pale flame leap from the muzzle.

A LEISURE BOOK®

March 2009

Published by special arrangement with Golden West Literary Agency.

Dorchester Publishing Co., Inc.
200 Madison Avenue
New York, NY 10016

ISBN 10: 0-8439-6173-2
ISBN 13: 978-0-8439-6173-7

The name "Leisure Books" and the stylized "L" with design are trademarks of Dorchester Publishing Co., Inc.

Printed in the United States of America.

10 9 8 7 6 5 4 3 2 1

Visit us on the web at www.dorchesterpub.com.

Destiny
Range

L. P. Holmes

LEISURE BOOKS NEW YORK CITY

DATE DUE

I

The thin file of riders moved slowly, for the dust of long miles and the shadow of fatigue lay heavy on both men and horses. Their way led north and east, angling upward across a tremendous, billowing slope of smoky grey sage and leaden green junipers. To the west that slope fell away into a gulf of distance calculated to stagger the eye: down and out until it seemed to fairly vanish in the curling mists of heat and sun haze. And those hard, eye-aching mists and the dancing haze eventually washed like a sea against the flanks of a jagged range of purple mountains which marched aloof and lonely along the far rim of the world. About the highest peaks of those mountains, bits of fleecy cloud clung.

Dexter Sublette twisted in his saddle, looked back at the four riders following him. One of those riders had a blood clotted bandage about his head. "How you making it, Chuck?" he asked.

"Good enough," answered Chuck Rollins. "I'm not seeing any spooks yet, but if I had to ride another million miles without a drink of water, I probably would be."

"Stay with it, cowboy. We'll hit the creek in another couple of miles."

They went on, saddle gear creaking, hoofs beating out a broken cadence, a thin haze of dust lifting and clinging about them in the motionless air. There was a grim, silent stoicism about the five men.

Imperceptibly the slope began to flatten and the horses moved more easily—faster. And in the sweep of the sage ahead a thin line of vivid green took form. It seemed that Chuck Rollins swayed slightly in the saddle as his feverish, blood-shot eyes picked up that line of green. Two of the rear riders swiftly lifted their horses to fast pace, moved up, one on each side of Chuck. Chuck grinned crookedly at each of them in turn.

"I'm all right, boys. I just got to thinking of the creek—and water."

"Stout fellah, Chuck," approved one of the cowboys.

As that line of vivid green came closer the horses increased their pace without urging. Equine throats knew the pang of thirst also. Soon the pace moved from a walk to a shuffling jog. The horses began tossing their heads eagerly.

The silent stoicism of the riders gave way to terse words. Shoulders straightened. "Anyhow," said Shorty Bartle—"I found out what the Thunder River Canyon looks like. Which is something."

"And I expect it will be a better canyon just because a bow-legged little squirt like you looked at it," taunted Dolf Andrews.

"Why not?" retorted Shorty. "It'll never be looked at by a better man. And that takes in you, my lantern jawed friend."

Up ahead, Dexter Sublette smiled grimly. His little crew was getting back to normal. Behind them lay hardship, fatigue, danger, disappointment. But it was not the nature of these men to dwell too much on the past, especially when they were young, like Shorty and Dolf. The intriguing vistas of life ahead held too much lure for them.

That line of green, a continuous thicket of choke cherry, willow and wild vines was just before them now. This was Concho Creek, rising far back in the low hills beyond the home ranch, to dawdle lazily across the flats and then, as though to make up for its laziness, tipped over the great sage slope and drove down in a straight line, on and on into the mists, to finally find junction with the foaming waters in the cold, barren depths of the Thunder River Canyon.

Dex Sublette reined in, stepped stiffly from the saddle. "Dolf, you and Shorty take the horses. Don't let them founder themselves. Wasatch, you help me with Chuck."

Chuck almost fell as he slid from his saddle. Dex took him by one arm, grizzled old Wasatch Lane by the other. They slid down the bank, fought a way through the tangle of willow and choke cherry and broke into a cool, shadowy cavern, down which the racing water tumbled and foamed.

"Flatten out, Chuck," said Dex. "I don't want you gulping at that water just yet. You got to cool off some."

Chuck sprawled out and Dex, scooping up a hatful of water, began splashing it over Chuck's face and head. Chuck gave a long, shuddering sigh of relief. Down below, brush was crashing and splintering as Dolf and Shorty brought in the horses.

Presently Dex let Chuck roll over and bury his face in the water, and when he saw that Chuck was not gorging himself, flattened out on his stomach and quenched his own thirst. Wasatch Lane, lifting a dripping face, grinned at Dex.

"Old bear has nothing on us," he drawled. "He went over the mountain. We went down it. We saw a lot of country, but no horse thieves, not even the one that creased Chuck. And we're out about twenty head of saddle stock. I'd shore like to know just where those broncs and the coyotes who rustled 'em, disappeared to, Dex."

Dex shrugged. "That's a big country, down around old Thunder. We didn't know the country, the rustlers did. There could be a thousand trails, and we wouldn't know any of them unless we just happened to stumble across one."

"Do you think it was Sawtelle who pulled the raid?"

"If I said so I'd be guessing. It might have been. But that Thunder River country is wild, Wasatch. I doubt if Sawtelle and his crowd are the only outlaw band who hang out there. And there is a possible chance that we're looking entirely too far from home."

Wasatch squinted thoughtfully, building a cigarette. "Meaning—Alviso?" he drawled.

Dex nodded. "But we're not saying so—yet. The best thing we can do for a time is to say nothing. We lost the horses. It is our affair. And if we don't spread our troubles you can never tell when something is liable to show up. How you feeling now, Chuck?"

"A heap better," sighed Chuck. "I got a hold on the world again. Things kind of stay in one place. But that last couple of miles—well, I wasn't shore whether I was forking a bronc or a dust devil. Twirl me one of those, will you, Wasatch?"

Wasatch spun another expert cigarette, tucked it into Chuck's mouth and scratched a sulphur match. Chuck inhaled gratefully.

Shorty came scrambling up over the foam lashed rocks. "Broncs are ready," he announced. "They didn't use up over half the creek. And that black, hammer-headed tarantula of yours, Wasatch—someday I'm going to iron a few of the kinks out of that brute's brain with a pick handle. He liked to trompled me to death, getting down to the water. Me—I don't savvy what you see in such a bronc."

"That bronc," averred Wasatch solemnly, though his deep eyes were twinkling—"is the best bronc ever foaled. He can out-run a antelope and he's got the bottom of a grizzly."

"And you're a liar by the clock," Shorty declared. "All the brute has is a disposition like a buzz-saw—just about on a par with yours. How's the coco, Chucky, m'lad?"

"Better," grinned Chuck. "I can travel any time."

"Then we ride," said Dex, getting to his feet. "For all we know we may be out of a job when we get home. The old ranch is bound to be sold one of these days, and the new owner may not like our looks or the way we part our hair—or the way we let valuable saddle stock be rustled right under our nose. I wouldn't blame 'em, at that."

"You would say something along that line," blurted Shorty. "Ain't my head bowed with shame, without you heaping on the coals?"

Dex chuckled. "You little wart. You're as empty headed as a sage wren. One thing you'll never suffer from is worry."

"Right as rain," declared Wasatch. "A man has to have brains to worry."

Back in the saddle once more, they turned almost due east, paralleling Concho Creek. And soon they were beyond the sage and the lip of the great slope and jogging along through grassy, rolling swells, where a smattering of white faced cattle began to show.

There had been more seriousness in Dex Sublette's reference to the possible sale of the Pinon Ranch than the other riders had guessed. He wished the thing would be settled, one way or another. Not knowing from day to day just who would sign the next pay check was enough to keep any thoughtful man on tenter-hooks.

Dex was young, himself—not much older than Dolf and Shorty, but there was a soberness, a solid, substantial streak in him which old Bill Ladley had recognized when he made Dex foreman of the spread. But age and ill-health had descended on Ladley in unison, forcing him to retire and seek medical advice in Phoenix. He had put the ranch up for sale, letting John Lockyear, an attorney in Holbrook, handle the deal. Since then there had been two prospective purchasers show up and look the ranch over, but neither of them had bought. Dex had not been able to understand this, unless they had wanted some kind of terms which Lockyear was not interested in. For the Pinon Ranch was as good a layout as could be found anywhere—plenty of range, of water, of shelter. And the price which Ladley was asking, twenty thousand dollars, was more than fair.

Shorty came spurring up even with Dex. "I been thinking," he said—"about the sale of the old spread. Do you think there is anything to that line of guff which Jake Enders was giving us, last week?"

Dex shook his head, grinning. "Jake was just pulling a come-on with you and Dolf, just to see your eyes pop."

"I'm not so shore of that, Dex. I know Jake and I know he loves to talk and that he's got what he calls a sense of humor. But he struck me as being real serious, like he was telling the truth for once in his life. He really had made a trip to Holbrook, you know. And he swears that Lockyear gave him a straight story."

"You said Enders was giving us a line of guff, Shorty. I think you were right the first time. Tell me this, why should a Russian Princess buy a cattle ranch in this country? It don't make sense."

"That's what I told Dolf, by golly," nodded Shorty. "The more you think of it, the taller it gets. Shucks! Princesses ain't interested in running any cattle ranch. All they do is sit on silk cushions, eat ice-cream and drink sody-pop. Enders shore must have been lying, after all. Me—I'm glad he was. I don't want to be working for no woman. They ain't got no idea of a man's strength. They run him around until he's nothing but skin and bones. Look at Bob Stickle, for instance. He used to be sort of plump. Now he's so thin he could hide behind a sand flea's whisker. And he's only been married about four years. Yes sir—women are slave drivers."

"To hear him talk," came Wasatch's twangy drawl—"you'd think he'd owned a harem at one time. What self-respecting woman would ever look at a runt like him? I ask you."

"Your ears," retorted Shorty sweetly—"are so danged long they would make a jack-ass lop-sided. Nobody was talking to you. When I want to tell you something, I'll draw a picture, so you'll be shore and understand."

Shorty dropped back beside Wasatch, to trade endless and scandalous insults. Shorty was irrepressible. He would argue over anything at any time. And the rest of the outfit loved him.

The riders broke clear of the shoulder of a low ridge and the buildings of the Pinon Ranch lay before them, grouped at the head of a pleasant little basin where a grove of cottonwoods swung away from the creek bed in semi-circular effect. The ranchhouse stood well back among the trees at the lip of a gentle slope which led down to the corrals, the bunkhouse, feed sheds and other buildings.

"I hope Hop has got some grub ready," exclaimed Shorty. "I'm hungry enough to eat a horned frog and not gag at the stickers."

They swung down and began unsaddling. A wrinkled, bright-eyed little Chinaman stepped out of the ranchhouse door and beat a clangor from a steel triangle hanging on a wire. Shorty whooped. "Me—I love that China boy like a blood brother. Any time, any where—you can bet on Hop having grub in the pot. Let go that bit, bronc. I got no time to argue."

They trooped around to the back door where Shorty and Dolf fought over the first chance at the wash basin. When they went in and sat down at the long, oil-cloth covered table, Hop brought Dex a long, legal looking envelope. Dex glanced at the return address. It was from John Lockyear. Dex frowned, hesitated and put the envelope aside unopened.

"Who brought it out, Hop?" he asked.

"Missy Doo—Doo—" Hop floundered over a name too much for his oriental tongue.

"Milly Duquesne, eh. Did you thank her?"

Hop nodded and grinned. "Give'm piece pie—cup coffee. She nice lady, Missy Doo—Doo—"

"Go easy, Hop—or you'll choke to death," advised Shorty. "Call her 'Brick' or 'Carrots' or something like that. Milly would probably knock your ears down if you did, but even that is better than choking to death. Who's that letter from, Dex?"

"Your grandfather, most likely," cut in Dolf. "And advising us to cut your throat before you talk us all to death. Dry up, and let a man handle his victuals."

The men ate hungrily. Even Chuck forgot his wounded head, for these men had been near eighteen hours without food and had ridden long and weary miles. But as the first edge of their hunger began to dull, more and more glances were thrown at that envelope which lay beside Dex Sublette's plate. And when the last generous wedge of Hop's famous pie had disappeared and cigarettes were alight, curiosity mounted rapidly.

Shorty Bartle, wriggling and squirming like an impatient bird dog, finally burst out. "For gosh sakes, Dex—open that letter and see what it says. I'll have the jimjams in another minute."

"I guess you'd better, Dex," drawled Wasatch—"else the runt will jiggle himself clear out of his pants."

Dex chuckled and opened the letter. As he read it his lean, sun-blackened face turned sober and thoughtful. He read it over again, leaned back and looked along the table. "The ranch is sold, boys," he said.

"I knew it," yelped Shorty. "I knew it. Who bought it, Dex?"

"Jake Enders told the truth. Boys—our new boss is a Russian Princess."

There was a long moment of stunned, almost horrified silence. Then Shorty moaned.

"Aw! Aw! This is the worst news I ever heard. A Russian Princess! I must be dreaming. Read it again, Dex. You made a mistake—you know you made a mistake. There's something wrong with your eyes. Read it again."

14

"No mistake, Shorty. It's here in cold black and white. And what's more, she'll be rolling into San Geronimo on the four o'clock overland. Which means I got to be moving. We all got to be moving. Shorty, you and Dolf get the buckboard hooked up—pronto. I've got to clean up and hoe these whiskers off. While I'm gone after her, you fellows all pitch in and help Hop Lee get the house cleaned up. Hop, you go over Bill Ladley's old room with a fine toothed comb. Make it fit for a lady to sleep in. Break out brand new blankets from the store-room. And all of you boys make use of a razor and dig some clean clothes out of your war-bags. You look like a flock of Comanche Indians. Fly to it, everybody."

"I thought I had hard luck when a bronc kicked in two ribs for me," Shorty groaned. "But I didn't know what hard luck was. A Russian Princess for a boss! Holy cow! If that ain't awful! I'll bet she'll be a string-necked old battle-axe, soured on the world—and the male sex in particular. I'll bet she'll take an unholy delight in raw-hiding us to a fare-ye-well. I'll bet—"

"You'll get your ears knocked down if you don't get a wiggle on," cut in Dex. "Get that buckboard ready and grease it for a change while you're at it. Scat!"

The dazed Shorty and Dolf departed at a run. Dex headed for the bunkhouse with Wasatch and Chuck. Dex glanced keenly at Chuck. "There's a touch of fever in your eyes, Chuck," he said. "That bad head of yours needs rest. You hit the hay and stay there until I say different."

Chuck would have demurred, but Dex cut him short. "No go, cowboy. You for the blankets. Wasatch, you clean that head up and put a fresh bandage on it."

Chuck stretched out on his bunk. Dex dragged out his war-bag. Wasatch started to strip the bandage from Chuck's head. He sighed heavily. "I might have known something like this would have to come along and ruin the peace of my old age. If you ask me, the old Pinon Ranch is in for plenty of misery. I've seen women take over the reins of a ranch before—and I never yet saw such an unlucky outfit turn for the better. Most usually it becomes a regular madhouse. And some of those women were western born and raised. Just imagine what we're in for. Or won't your imagination reach that far?"

"That sounds like Shorty talking," said Dex.

"Well, it's not," growled Wasatch. "This is Wasatch Lane orating—Wasatch Lane, who's grown old and weary watching the mistakes of a misfit world. Now comes the final blow. Me—I got a good notion to draw my time and light a shuck out of here. I'm getting too old to change my ways and this princess person is shore to have more cussed reforms up her sleeve than you can shake a stick at. Yes sir, I got a hunch that Wasatch Lane better pack his bag and hit the trail."

Dex, laying out his shaving kit, grinned. "You'll do nothing of the sort, you frowsy old badger. You'll stick around and help me make the grade. You and the other boys got nothing to worry about. Me—being foreman, will be the one to catch all the trouble. And

16

now listen to me. You be sure and see that Hop and the boys do a good job of swamping out the house. None of this lick and a promise stuff. I want it scrubbed. Also, before I get back, have Shorty or Dolf take the shears and roach your hair. You look like a porcupine."

Wasatch Lane's eyes twinkled. All his mournful talk of pulling out was nothing but sham. There wasn't a force in the world, outside of death itself, which could have torn the old fellow from the side of Dex Sublette. He loved the boy like a father loves a son. The trail they had ridden together had been a long one, fruitful with the danger and hardship which, when shared side by side, welds strong men together in a deep, quiet affection that nothing can break. And Dexter Sublette knew that where he was, there would Wasatch Lane always be.

"All right," groaned Wasatch. "Have it your own way. But you'll see I'm right. This is no country for a foreign princess. This country was made for men with fur on their chests. You got to be able to live on sow-bosom and beans to get along in this country."

Dex spat out a mouthful of foamy lather and began stropping his razor. "All you know about royal ladies is what you've read in fairy stories, old settler. I think I understand the idea of this new boss of ours. You know, since the big war, thrones and titles haven't been worth four-bits a dozen over there in Europe. A lot of royal families are plumb busted—especially in Russia.

"Jake Enders was telling me that he remembers this lady. Years ago she was out in this neck of the woods with her daddy on a hunting trip. She was just a little girl, then. They made head-quarters here at the Pinon Ranch back when Bill Skagway owned and ran it. Chances are, this lady never forgot the old ranch. Royal folks went through tough times during that Russian revolution. Probably she saved enough out of the wreck to buy this ranch, where she figures to settle down in peace and quiet and forget Russia for good. I'll bet she's pretty darn sensible. Otherwise she wouldn't have bought a good ranch, darned reasonable."

"Well, maybe," grunted Wasatch grudgingly. "Maybe she is. I shore as hell hope so. What's her name, anyhow? Or didn't Lockyear put it in that letter?"

Dex took another look at the letter, which he laid upon his bunk. "S-o-n-i-a-," he spelled out slowly. "Sonia Stephens. Used to be Sonia Stephanovich. I guess that's the way you pronounce it. But she's evidently going to be a good American. Changed her name to plain Stephens, already."

"That's something in her favor," agreed Wasatch. "Leave that razor out when you get done. I'll scrape my face and have Dolf roach my mane. Then I'll see that Hop and the boys do a real job on the big house."

Dolf and Shorty had the buckboard ready to roll when Dex came out. Dex had donned his best shirt and a brand new blue silk scarf. Shorty sniffed disdainfully. "Look at him. All slicked up like a bronc with a braided tail. The bright star of the freedom of men is beginning to fade. I can see that cloud of slavery coming over the hills. We won't be able to take a shot of honest liquor, we'll have to sneak down behind the feed sheds to smoke a cigarette. We'll be tying nice silk ribbons on the horns of every steer under our brand and if we slam a slick too hard when we're branding we'll catch merry hell, with a lecture on cruelty to animals thrown in for good luck. We'll have to file our spurs, throw away our guns. Dex—old boy, if you love me—do me a favor, will you?"

Dex, laughing softly, stepped into the buckboard and picked up the reins. "What'll it be, runt?"

"If she's one of these reforming kind, you know what I mean—the kind with a long nose and sharp eyes, the kind that look right down into a man's vitals and tell him he's a sinful, no good cross between a worm and a pale jackrabbit—don't bring her out here."

"I got to bring her out," chuckled Dex. "She owns this ranch now, and we're working for her. What she says goes, from now on."

"You might stage a runaway," offered Shorty hopefully—"and either scare her to death or chuck her out in the rocks and break her neck. There's more than one way to skin a cat, you know."

"I'll skin you with this horse-whip in a minute," threatened Dex. "Sand it up to the house, grab a scrubbing brush and get to work. If that house don't shine when I get back, I'll show you what real misery is like."

As soon as Dex swung the buckboard out into the

narrow, twisting road which led to San Geronimo, fourteen miles distant, all the levity went out of his face and manner. He grappled with serious thought. The future was even more uncertain now than it had been before. True, the ranch had finally found a buyer—but such a buyer!

Dex knew the language of cattlemen. He could hold his own with men at any time, in any way. But women—well, outside of Milly Duquesne, whom he'd known for years and with whom he had always fought, for Milly had red hair and the temper of a bear-cat, Dex had had little experience with women, least of all with a former Russian Princess.

This was a hard fact to swallow. It seemed almost unreal—almost impossible. Added to the strangeness was the fact that this alien purchaser had bought virtually blindly, taking the word of John Lockyear fully.

True, from what Dex had heard, this princess had visited the Pinon Ranch when a little girl, back in Bill Skagway's time. Dex calculated swiftly. Shucks! That wouldn't make her so old, not a day older than Dex himself, who had seen twenty-five summers drift by. Yes sir—she'd be young. And at best she wouldn't be able to remember much about the ranch. She would probably be disappointed, as Dex knew from experience was so often the case. A person was apt to paint something in the past with too glowing a color and on revisiting old scenes find them narrower and smaller than they could possibly imagine. It didn't always pay to go back over cold trails.

Dex pushed his hat to the back of his head and ruffed his tawny hair reflectively. He tried to imagine what this princess would look like. He thought of Shorty's scathing statements and the doubts and fears of Wasatch. He grinned. It would be a swell joke on both of them if this Sonia Stephens turned out to be a handsome little monkey and possessed of a good level head besides. If such was the case, would Shorty and Wasatch have to eat crow!

Buying blind, the way she had done, seemed to Dex like a sentimental gesture. She had probably known a lot of trouble and sorrow in her own country and wanted to get away where she could forget it all, where she could live her own life in her own way. And she had changed her name, which, Dex reflected, made it pretty certain that she was going to be a good American.

His thoughts switched to the Pinon ranchhouse, where by this time Wasatch and Hop and the other boys would be scrubbing and mopping furiously. Dex wished he'd had a little more time to work at that house. It was a pretty good house, as ranchhouses went. It was roomy and soundly built. But it had long been a bachelor domain and busy ranch owners of the bachelor sort did not spend much time figuring out comforts and furniture for a house. He hoped that Wasatch and the boys did not forget to look into the dark corners.

This new owner would probably fix the old house up a lot. Women put much store in a tidy, comfortable house with a lot of colorful gee-gaws and such things. She'd probably put curtains at the windows and want a little flower garden out in front. Women were strong for window curtains and flower gardens. And there would be a lot of painting to do. Women were great on paint, so he'd heard Bob Stickle say—and Bob sure had ought to know—for as Shorty would say, Bob Stickle was a plenty married man.

Dex glanced at the sun, then snapped the whip, which caused the stout little team of broncos to let out another link of speed. Even if the overland was right on time and they could get away from San Geronimo without delay, it would be quite a while after dark before getting back to the ranch. Maybe this princess would want to put up at the hotel for the night and drive out in the morning. She probably would, which meant that Dex would have to drive another round trip in the morning. Dex sighed. Maybe Shorty was right, after all.

The road curled away through the junipers and past spreads of sage and sour grass. Here the country had a gentle, rolling, up and down tempo, which put a man on the top of a low ridge one moment, where his eye might reach for miles, then dropped him to a hollow the next, where he could see nothing but an immediate area of a few hundred yards. And as the buckboard topped another of those ridges, Dex jerked erect in the seat and stared ahead with eyes that narrowed and turned a little cold. Ahead, swinging up out of a dry arroyo and into the road, were four riders. The leader of the four bestrode a spirited looking bay gelding and his riding rig was bright and heavy with silver inlay. The riders pulled in beside the road and waited.

Dex edged the big Colt gun at his hip to a slightly more handy position and rolled up to them. The rider of the bay gelding swung the horse athwart the road and Dex had to rein in.

"What is this, Alviso," demanded Dex curtly. "A hold-up?"

Don Diego Alviso had the leathery swarthiness of his race, but he was a distinctly handsome man with regular, aquiline features, black eyes, and a tiny, pointed mustache. His clothes were as ornate and expensive as his riding rig. His shirt was of the sheerest white silk, his scarf of the same material but a robin's egg blue in color. His short bolero jacket was of black velvet, heavy with braid, and his trousers, of the same material, were tight about his hips, but flared wide at the bottom of each leg, the slash inset with crimson. His boots were of the softest calfskin and his spurs almost solid silver, with tremendous, cruel rowels. His sombrero, with a high, sugar-loaf crown, was of heavy, expensive quilted felt—black with a cord of braided silver around it. About his waist was a gunbelt of black calfskin, laced with white buckskin, and the twin guns hanging at his thighs in carved, open topped holsters, were ivory handled. The silver chin thong of his sombrero, looked almost white against the darkness of his skin.

At the curtness of Dex Sublette's tone, the Spaniard's black eyes narrowed and moiled, but he smiled slightly, showing even white teeth.

"But no, amigo," he protested. "Why should I hold up you? We are good neighbors, no? I would merely speak with you of one or two small matters."

"Speak up, then," growled Dex. "I'm in a hurry."

"First, I would request that you keep that breed bull of yours somewhere else but on my range, senor. But yesterday that big ruffian was on my range where he gored two of my bulls so badly I had to order them killed. I dislike to speak of such a small matter, but—" The Don shrugged his sleek shoulders and turned the palms of his hands upward.

"So old Blitzen is on the rampage again, eh," nodded Dex. "I'll set the boys out tomorrow to round him up and drift him far enough back on our east range, he never will find your place again. As for your two bulls, if you will show me the hides and your price is right, I'll pay the damage."

The smile on the Don's face became queerly set. There was not the slightest mirth in it. And his voice grew a trifle more marked with accent.

"You would see the hides—you do not trust my word?"

It was on the tip of Dex Sublette's tongue to tell this fellow that far from taking his word for anything, it was his opinion that Don Diego Alviso was a bombastic, overdressed, lying, double-crossing coyote. But such an outburst at this time was almost certain to precipitate quite a jog of trouble, which might delay his trip to San Geronimo. And Dex felt that he had serious business in town. So he said the diplomatic thing.

"Just a matter of business, that's all, Alviso. It would be the money of the owner of the Pinon Ranch I'd be paying for those two bulls of yours—and when I spend money that belongs to someone else, I make sure I know all the details."

The Don relaxed slightly and the set expression about his mouth smoothed out a trifle. He built a thin, husk cigarette, twirling it deftly to shape with his brown, tapered fingers. "It has come to my ears," he purred—"that the Pinon Ranch is to have a new owner—a lady, a foreign lady of noble birth. Is there any truth in those words, Senor?"

Dex's jaw stole out. Now he knew why the Don had stopped him. That talk about the gored bulls was all a lie, just as he had expected. The Spaniard was looking for information about this Russian Princess—the Pinon Ranch princess—his princess, by gollies. So Dex's gray eyes became bits of frosty shadow.

"That," he said distinctly—"is none of your damn business. Get off the road, Alviso—or I'll run over you."

With the words, Dex lifted his whip, cut the two broncos smartly and they lunged forward at a run. The Don just did swing his horse aside in time, but he got full benefit of the dust thrown up by hoof and wheel.

For a little distance Dex drove with his chin on his shoulder. You had to watch these spigs, he thought savagely. Be just like them to shoot a man in the back, especially when they were of the stripe of Alviso and his collection of coffee colored renegades. But no shot followed Dex and, as the buckboard swept over the next rise ahead, Dex caught a distant glance of the town of San Geronimo, out there in the plains, lazy and sleepy in the late afternoon sunshine. Also, dim as an echo out of the northeast, came the thin, far wail of a train whistle.

Dex used the whip on the broncos again. He'd be just about in time.

II

She came down the steps of the dusty overland coach a little stiffly, as though the long ride across a continent had wearied her. Yet, despite the confines of a Pullman compartment, her trig little dove gray traveling suit and snug, close fitting turban hat of the same shade, looked crisp and unwrinkled.

As she straightened up, her head lifted proudly, almost imperiously, and in the dark eyes which calmly surveyed the weather-beaten railroad station at San Geronimo was a look that made Salty Simmons, the fat, good-natured agent, turn to Dex Sublette with a little whistle of admiration.

"It's true, Dex," blurted Salty. "Shore, I didn't take much stock in all the rumor folks have been spreading that there was a real, honest-to-grandma foreign Princess coming to live at the Pinon ranch—but I believe it, now. Doggoned if I don't feel like bowing and scraping to her like some gosh-blamed butler."

Dex nodded soberly. "I get what you mean, Salty. She's the pure quill. She's royal, all right. And now I got to go up and introduce myself. I'm scared plumb silly. How do you go about greeting a princess, Salt?"

"I ain't never met one," said Salty honestly. "I reckon all you can do is go up and say 'Howdy, Princess— how's things?' Ain't that about right?"

"It sounds kinda sudden to me. But here goes. I can't stand here gawking at her like a locoed sheep-herder. Wish me luck, Salt."

Dex left Salty's side and stalked across the platform, his spur chains tinkling. The new arrival looked at him and, for a moment, her dark eyes and his gray ones met and clung. And Dex made a startling discovery. Her eyes were not black, as he had first thought, but of such a deep, deep shade of blue as to appear almost purple.

Her face was a delicate oval, slightly high of cheekbone. Her skin was a dusky, smooth ivory. Her lips were bewitching. The lower one was particularly full and rich and crimson, and it gave to her expression an elfin impudence which was a delight. Here and there, from beneath the edges of her hat, a few threads of black, silken hair showed. She made an absorbing, stirring picture as she stood there, half defiantly, half appealingly.

On her part, Sonia Stephens, born to the royal purple, but transplanted by the searing touch of war and brutal revolution and disaster to the strange surroundings of the far flung western plains of America, found herself surveying a tall, wide-shouldered, lean flanked young

27

fellow, whose hair gleamed tawny as the sun mellowed grass beneath the wide brim of his pushed back Stetson sombrero. His face was lean and brown, clear cut and strong of feature. Her gaze lingered for a moment on his face, dropped to where his gunbelt sagged about his hips, then lifted to his face once more. Dex took off his hat and bowed slightly.

"Pardon, Ma'am—were you looking for the foreman of the Pinon Ranch?"

"Yes. I am Sonia Stephens. Are you Dexter Sublette?"

Dex liked her voice. It was low and a little throaty, with an appealing husky note. And there was just a hint of attractive accent, though her diction was perfect.

"I am," he nodded. "I'm here to take you out to the ranch, unless you intend to stay over night here in San Geronimo."

"I wish to go directly to my ranch," she said quickly.

"That's fine," Dex enthused. "I got the buckboard tied over yonder. Soon as I load your luggage, we'll be rolling."

She smiled and nodded, turning back to the train, where a porter was lugging down several traveling bags. And as the last bag came in sight, Dex got another surprise. A plump, demure, sparkling-eyed young lady stepped down and advanced to the side of Sonia Stephens.

"That is all of the hand bags, your highness," she announced. "The trunks are being unloaded from the baggage car."

Sonia Stephens nodded, turning again to Dex. "This is my maid, Marcia—Mr. Sublette."

Marcia favored Dex with a dimpled smile as she curtsied prettily. "I am so pleased," she murmured.

Dex bowed again, and to cover his bewilderment, beckoned the round eyed Salty Simmons. "Help me load this baggage, will you, Salt," he muttered. "Here's an angle I didn't expect. She's brought a maid with her."

Salty mumbled something and grabbed up an armful of hand bags which he lugged around to the buckboard, Dex following with the remainder. For a moment or two they were out of earshot of the women.

"Holy cow!" panted Salty. "Got me a notion to drift over to this Russia country. Never saw two such good looking women in my life. Wonder if they're all like those two."

"Darned if I know," Dex growled. "One woman out at the old Pinon outfit would mean trouble. Two of them will tear the place to pieces. Think, Salty—just think what it will mean to have those two women at the ranch. Why, when the word spreads around, every damned romantic cow-punch in a hundred miles will be hanging around. I'll bet Dolf and Shorty go boggle-eyed over that Marcia critter the minute they get a look at her. They won't be worth shucks around the place. And tell me this, Salt—how in blazes am I going to haul all these hand bags and those four trunks, plus myself and two women in this one lone buckboard?"

Salty grinned. "I'll trade places with you, Dex. It ain't every jasper is lucky enough to make a fifteen mile drive or thereabouts, with a couple of high class women like those two. You should worry over the baggage. You can haul that out in the chuck wagon."

"That's what I'll have to do, I reckon," said Dex. "I'll take along the hand bags and send one of the boys in tomorrow with the chuck wagon to get the trunks. Hold the broncs until we get set, Salt. Ah—this way, ladies. We'll have to leave the trunks, Boss—and send for them tomorrow. Will that be all right?"

"Of course," nodded Sonia Stephens. She smiled. "You did not expect such a load?"

"No—I didn't," Dex drawled. "But we'll make out all right. Anything you want, Boss—before we start? It's quite a drive. It will be after dark before we get there. Have you eaten lately?"

The smile grew, showing a row of sparkling teeth. "We had something just before the train arrived. I know of nothing to keep us here. And I am very anxious to get to my ranch."

"Fair enough," said Dex. "Up you go."

The buckboard step was rather high and Sonia looked at it doubtfully. Dex proved equal to the occasion. He caught her by the elbows and tossed her lightly up. She gasped and colored and looked at him with fathomless glance. "You—you are—rather abrupt, Mr. Dexter Sublette."

Suddenly at his ease, Dex turned to the maid and lifted her up beside her mistress. Then he climbed in himself, unwound the reins, kicked off the brake and nodded to Salty.

"Turn 'em loose, Salt," he drawled.

The eager, fretting broncos whirled away from the hitching rail, spun the buckboard around at such a precarious angle that Sonia Stephens caught at Dex's arm, then whipped off down the street in a whistle of slithering wheels and weaving jets of dust. A wide-eyed, envious Salty Simmons watched them go.

A spanking mile took the first edge off the broncos and the shaggy little animals settled down to a steady, swinging pace. Dex relaxed and looked down at the turbaned head at his shoulder. Three on the none too wide seat made a rather snug fit and Dex was disconcertedly conscious of the warm pressure of her slim figure. "I'm sorry there ain't more room," he apologized. "I hope you are comfortable."

She looked up at him, her lips grave, but with a sparkle of mischief lighting the depths of those amazing eyes. "Thank you. I am glad I am so close to you. If these horses should run away, I could cling to you. Of course, if you like, I'll have Marcia ride on the baggage."

"Gosh no!" exploded Dex. "I'm all right. This is great—I mean—well, I just wanted to be shore that everything was all right."

Dex wondered furiously as to why his tongue should be so confoundedly clumsy. Just because this girl had a voice full of haunting magic and eyes like some purple, exotic sea, was no reason for him to act like some clumsy tongued jackass. He had to get a grip on himself, or she wouldn't think him man enough to run her ranch for her.

She was speaking again. "You might remove that huge weapon from this side. I'm afraid it might explode. Is it necessary to carry a gun like that all the time?"

Dex removed the offending .45 from the holster and shoved it down inside the waist band of his overalls. "I don't pack it for looks or because I like the weight," he answered gravely.

"That," she said—"is evading the question. This country is so wide and still and peaceful. Where, and against what, would you use such a weapon?"

Dex pointed ahead with his whip. "There's a lot of things in that country that you can't see right now, Ma'am. You're still thinking in terms of law and order because less than half an hour ago you stepped out of a train. But that train is just the edge of things. When we turned our backs to it, we turned our faces to a country that is awful big, awful wild, and at times—plenty tough. Within the next week I'll show you country that will make your heart stand still. I'll show you country so big and raw that it will scare you. And that kind of country always holds—well—things that a gun is the only argument against. By the time you've been here a month, you'll carry a gun yourself, whenever you are out of your own ranchhouse."

"Heavens! I never shot a gun in my life. I'm horribly afraid of them."

"I'll teach you how to use one," said Dex. "A gun is valuable insurance—in this country."

She laughed a trifle uncertainly. "Why should anyone wish to bother with me? Since I bought my ranch I have very little money. Certainly no one would get rich, robbing me."

Dex glanced at her profile. "You are," he said slowly—"a strikingly beautiful young woman. There are many men in this country who never saw a woman like you. I never had—until today. And some of those men are wild and rough and uncertain."

The color washed up into her face. "You speak," she said—"with a gravity beyond your years, Dexter Sublette."

"I am twenty-five," he said. "And this country has a way of putting weight into the years that a man lives here. Things are what they are, out here and fundamentals are the only things that count. If you try and laugh 'em off, you don't last long."

"You make it sound very stern and savage," she murmured.

"It is," said Dex simply.

Marcia peeked across in front of her mistress. "Perhaps you shoot—Indians?" she asked.

Dex laughed, then. "Not any more. For that matter, we don't shoot anything, if we can help it. But we never know when we might have cause to start in. And if you need a gun, it don't do you a bit of good if you haven't got it with you."

A silence followed, broken only by the thud of the

broncos' hoofs and the grind of steel shod wheels cutting over some rocky place in the winding, dust clogged road. The sun was well down toward the horizon, now—firing long, slanting lances at the violet shadows which were beginning to spring up in every low spot and arroyo. South and west, misty with cool, blue shadows, the Thunderhead Mountains forked the far sky. And the air was crisping up, whipping color into soft cheeks and throats. The eyes of Sonia Stephens were glowing with the wonder and appreciation of it all.

"Like it?" asked Dex.

"It—it is glorious," she replied, a little breathlessly. "What is that scent—that pungent, tangy flavor in the air? It makes my throat smart, but I love it."

"Sage," said Dex—"sage and juniper. We'll get into it proper after we cross Sunken Wash. This wind is sweeping over a hundred miles of it. I've seen it at night when it is so strong it nearly strangles you. But it is good medicine. It will make you strong."

She wiggled an arm free and pointed. "Those mountains—they look so far and cold and lonely. What are they called?"

"The Thunderhead Mountains. Wait until you see a storm break over them. Then you'll understand how they got their name. I've seen the clouds bury them, and then there would be lightning which would blind you and thunder which would break your ears. One of those storms have a way of making a person feel kind of small and shivery and spooky. They do, for a fact."

"Thunder and lightning frightens me to death," she said. "But it fascinates me, too. It appeals to something in me that is wild and untamed."

Dex chuckled. "You don't look wild and untamed to me. You look the most proper, high class little person I ever laid eyes on."

She darted a slanting glance at him. "You haven't seen me in one of my moods," she warned. "Wait until you do."

Dex did not answer. He was staring out ahead and the whimsical humor had left his face, his expression turning harsh and set. Startled, she followed his glance and saw, drawn up beside the road, four riders. Stirred by the bleakness and couched ferocity in Dex Sublette's eyes, she was, for the moment, speechless.

Dex flicked the broncos to a faster pace and his right hand stole toward the butt of the gun he had stuck in the waist band of his jeans.

"What—who are they?" asked Sonia.

Dex's answer startled her still more. "Don't look at them," he said harshly. "Keep your eyes straight ahead."

"But," she argued—"I do not understand."

"I do—plenty," he told her curtly. "It would be just like that smooth pole-cat to wait out here. But," he added—as though to himself—"if he's gambling on an introduction, he's crazy."

Sonia, half bewildered, half angry at the tone and manner of this man beside her, did not obey Dex's instructions. She let her gaze run curiously over the four riders as the buckboard moved even with them and passed them. They were swarthy, these four, three of them looking rough and brutal. The fourth, riding a magnificent horse and dressed in gaudy splendor, swept off a wide sombrero and bowed low over his saddle horn, though his black eyes, peering upward, never missed a feature in his half impudent survey of the two women. And there were white teeth gleaming in a mocking smile, beneath a crisp, black mustache. Then the buckboard was past the four and skirling swiftly along.

Sonia glanced up at Dexter Sublette again. The bleakness was still in his face and the flush of anger staining his jaw.

"What a picturesque man that was," she murmured.

"Any pole-cat wears a gaudy coat," snapped Dex. "But that doesn't keep it from being—a pole-cat. You would have to look at him, of course."

Sonia stiffened under the gruff reproof. "My eyes are my own—to use as I wish," she said coolly.

"Keno," growled Dex. "Forget it."

They fell silent, after that. Sonia was well aware that in meeting the glance of that man back there beside the road, she had violated some strange standard of this new and mysterious world she had moved to. Just why she should have been guilty of wrong because she had merely glanced at a strange man with no more real interest than she would if looking at an animal, she could not understand. Different standards existed in different parts of the world, but this was one of the strangest of the strange. And she had succeeded in making this lean jawed fellow beside her if not angry, at least annoyed with her. The devils of mischief flickered, far back in her eyes. She drew upon her wiles.

"May I ask," she cooed—"just why I have done something wrong?"

"Not so much wrong—as foolish," stated Dex curtly. "To some people a casual glance is an invitation. Don Diego Alviso is just the sort to gamble that way."

"Don Diego Alviso," she murmured. "Then he is a nobleman?"

"Nobleman—hell!" exploded Dex. "He's an oily, lying mongrel, not fit to breathe air in the same world with such as you."

"You would—swear at me?" she demanded, with mock severity, though her eyes were dancing.

Dex shrugged. "I'm sorry. But sight of that hombre always makes me cuss. You don't understand."

She laughed then, very softly and her cheek brushed against his shoulder. "I am sorry to have upset you so, Dexter Sublette," she said with startling naïveté.

Dex smiled grudgingly. A clever little minx, this Russian Princess.

The sun went down. Dusk was swift and darkness right at its heels. The air grew colder. Marcia, who held a wrap in her arms, offered it to her mistress. "It grows cold, your highness. You will chill."

Dex pulled the broncos to a halt. "That will leave you without a wrap. You put that on. I'll take care of the boss."

He untied his folded sheepskin coat from the back of the buckboard seat and shook it out. "Crawl into this, boss. It will keep you cozy."

She laughed softly again, but obeyed, snuggling down into the turned up collar with a little shiver of contentment. As they resumed their way she looked up at him with another of those swift, side-long glances. "But you—you will suffer now, Dexter Sublette."

Dex shrugged. "Don't mind me. I'm used to it. Tell you what—I would like to roll a smoke—if you don't mind."

"Why of course." She added softly—"This coat—I like it. It smells so mannish, of tobacco smoke—and I am as warm as toast. Thank you."

Dex looked down at a face which seemed flower-like against the wide, wool ruff of the collar. "I want you to be comfortable. Nothing is too good for the boss of the Pinon Ranch."

She laughed then. "Boss—you call me boss. That is funny. I was never called boss, before."

"Better get used to it, then," grinned Dex, his good humor returned. He built a deft, one-handed smoke. "You'll hear it a lot."

He cupped a flaring match in the hollow of his hands and lifted it to the cigarette. The girl, watching him closely, saw the light etch his lean, strong features into glowing bronze. Somehow, she thought of an eagle. Dex pinched out the match and the darkness closed in again, broken only by the red tip of the cigarette which glowed and faded as he inhaled at intervals.

Abruptly a shrill yammering broke out on the far bank of Sunken Wash, which they were now crossing. Marcia squealed and clung to her mistress, who in turn pressed a little closer to Dex. Dex's easy laugh sounded.

"Coyote," he explained. "Desert pup. Yowling for God only knows what. I like to hear 'em. They won't hurt you."

Marcia was not entirely convinced. "It—it sounded like there was a hundred of them."

"That's a way they have," said Dex. "One of 'em, when it is really on the howl, can make you think the night is crawling with the brutes. But the howl is all there is to them. I'll bet that rascal, soon as it gets a whiff of us, will nearly set itself on fire, burning the wind out of here."

"I—I hope so," shivered Marcia.

Dex could feel the pressure of the slim figure increase against his shoulder. "It is foolish," Sonia murmured. "But even I—am half afraid. Everything is so big, so black, so tremendous. That wind even—it makes me lonely. Yet it all fascinates. Am I foolish?"

"No," said Dex gravely—"no, you're not. I know exactly what you mean. I was born in this kind of country—lived all my life in it—yet I get the same feeling about it. Only it doesn't scare me any more. It does something else. It gets hold of me—inside, and it lifts me up and makes me glad that I am alive—and that I'm here, in the midst of it all. There is something about it that is rich and fine—and terrific. I can't explain it. But it is something that grips you—and makes you content.

"I remember one time I had the offer of a job—a good job, as cattle buyer for a big packing outfit. It wouldn't have taken me entirely off the range, but it would have meant a lot of time in towns and on trains. I wouldn't have been in the saddle regularly any more. I wouldn't have had the smoke of a branding fire in my eyes, I wouldn't have been fogging through the dust of a trail herd any more. I went out alone, on a long ride over the range at night, to think the proposition out. And the night and the darkness—the wind and the stars got hold of me and spoke the old, old truths. And well—I'm still riding the range. Money isn't everything."

He could feel her nod. "Nor is fame, nor power, nor position, Dexter Sublette. I know that—oh, how I know that. And you have made me feel better. I will try and understand your night and your wind and your stars. Perhaps they will teach me peace, also."

These were strange words she spoke to Dex, with a wistful, plaintive melancholy in them. Dex heard her sigh, as though the weight of dark memories were upon her.

The miles reeled backward. The coyote yammered again and others in the far distance took up the wild, lonely chorus. The buckboard was in the sage and junipers now, dark masses of it reeling monotonously by on either side. The pungent smell of it was raw and tonic and seemed to lay on the tongue like some rich and aromatic oil.

Gradually that soft pressure against Dex's shoulder increased. He looked down. Her face was shadowy, sunk deep in the collar of the coat. Dex bent his head slightly. Her breathing was deep and soft and regular. She was asleep.

With infinite care Dex twisted about, his right arm going about her in a strong, gentle cradle. She relaxed inside it like a weary child, her cheek dropping forward against the front of his shirt. Marcia, the maid, was a humped up little bundle at the other end of the seat, nodding and dozing to herself. Imperceptibly Dex tightened his arm about the princess. She seemed to snuggle closer to him, a weary soul seeking a haven of strength and security.

Dex stared straight ahead into the night, his face grave and sober. He knew somehow that this was not merely a girl of dazzling looks, driven by wayward fancy into buying a cattle ranch. Somewhere along the back trail this lovely little youngster had been hurt, disillusioned. She had come to this western country to seek forgetfulness, to find a new life in a new world. She would need help and understanding, at those times when her courage might run out.

Sonia Stephens did not remember falling asleep. She knew that the long train ride had wearied her. And though the first miles of the trip out from San Geronimo had stimulated her by their newness and novelty, the soporific effect of the swaying, scudding buckboard had come upon her insidiously. This, coupled with the darkness and the enveloping warmth of

Dexter Sublette's coat, had made her a victim of sleep before she realized it.

She awoke, to find herself cradled in a pair of strong muscular arms, being carried like a child. For a moment a gust of startled fright set her up taut and shivering and an involuntary murmur of protest broke from her lips. Dexter Sublette's quiet, musical drawl came down to her.

"Easy does it, boss. You're all right. You were such a weary, sound asleep little trick I didn't have the heart to wake you up. In another jiffy you'll be sitting warm and pretty in your own ranchhouse."

She knew she shouldn't allow this. No man had ever carried her in his arms before. And the thought of an old legend flashed through her drowsy brain—something about the significance of being carried by a man across the threshold. . . . Her heart was throbbing a little wildly.

A burst of light struck her eyes and then there were four walls about her. She was lowered into a big, comfortable chair before the crackling flames of a rock built fire-place. She looked up and met Dex Sublette's grave, thoughtful eyes. He smiled.

"There you are, boss. Right in your own home, now. You had quite a snooze. You must have been tired out. But Hop will have something hot for you to eat and drink in a minute." He raised his voice. "Hop—you Hop—get a wiggle on, or I'll peel your yellow heathen hide with a bull whip."

Hop Lee, his beady eyes shining with excitement,

shuffled into the room. "Light away, Boss Dex—light away," he chirruped. "Ketchum pie and coffee fo' ladies."

Sonia said nothing, but her eyes were strange. She was half piqued with herself that she should have fallen asleep the way she did. She knew what it meant to have been asleep on that narrow buckboard seat. No sleeping person could have sat upright on that seat without being held that way. And there was but one person who could have held her there—Dexter Sublette.

She stole another swift glance at him. There, on the right breast of his shirt was a faint dusting of powder, where a woman's cheek might have rested. Color built up in her face. That dusting of powder had rubbed from her cheek. It had been her head which had rested there. She had slept within the circle of his supporting arm. And he had ended up by carrying her across the threshold of this ranchhouse. As she realized all this there was in her the mingled tumult of pique and anger and the faintest of insurgent thrill. What must he think of her?

But this big, bronzed young cowboy seemed totally at his ease and without embarrassment. His very casualness irritated her somehow. At least the big ruffian should have the grace to appear a little ashamed for his freedom with her regal person.

Then she was honest enough to realize the kindness and gentle thoughtfulness behind his act, so she said nothing. Besides, the heat of the fire was so welcome and the embrace of the chair so comfortable, she could not bring herself to any lasting state of indignation.

She shucked herself of Dex's coat and removed her tight little turban hat. Thus released, her hair fell about her shoulders in a gleaming, blue-black mass. She looked around for Marcia and saw that vivacious individual engaged in conversation with two bechapped, gun carrying savages.

She was about to speak sharply, but Dex fore-stalled her with a quick gesture. "Don't," he murmured. "Marcia is giving Dolf and Shorty the thrill of their misspent lives."

"But my hair," objected Sonia. "It is in a terrible state. I want Marcia to put it up for me."

Dex shook his head, his gray eyes unreadable. "Leave it that way. It's gorgeous, boss. It reminds me of the Thunderhead Mountains, full of lure and mystery."

Sonia grew a trifle panicky. What kind of men inhabited this wild land she had come to? True, she had been here once before in her life, but that had been long ago as a youngster, when she had accompanied her father to this American West, while he hunted. Naturally, her recollections were somewhat vague. But after the return to Russia she had heard her father often speak of these western Americans, and it had always been with admiration for the honest, fearless directness of them.

Now that beloved father was gone, shot down by a ratlike horde of revolutionists not fit to polish his aristocratic boots, but here were these same western men—direct, outspoken and honest. A little too much so, in fact, for Sonia's peace of mind. She welcomed the interruption of Hop Lee as he moved a small table up before her and set out steaming coffee and generous wedges of pie. On his part, Dex noticed that this slim, lovely, regal young creature left her gorgeous hair as he had requested.

Dex turned to the enamored Dolf and Shorty. "That young lady is probably half starved, boys. Suppose you postpone your little gab-fest until some other time. Come over here and meet your new boss."

Red of face and uncomfortable, Dolf and Shorty faced Sonia and bowed awkwardly. "Pleased to meet'cha, ma'am," they parroted together. "We shore are happy to be working for you."

They gulped at the beauty of the smile they received, and floundered awkwardly out of the room. "You want to look out for those two jaspers, Marcia," chuckled Dex. "They're regular heart-breakers."

Marcia indulged in a purely feminine giggle. "They are so funny—and nice. I like them."

Sonia felt that something had to be done about this free and easy camaraderie that was springing up. It was foreign to anything she had ever experienced before. Practically all her life she had moved through a circle of dignity and strict deportment. Even after the revolution the training of her early years had preserved that dignity. And now, even she, who had sat in regal functions at the right hand of her father, a grand duke high in royal favor, had allowed herself to be persuaded in a nicety of toilette by this towering, keen eyed fellow who was teasing Marcia.

"That will be enough, Marcia," said Sonia coldly. "You will refresh yourself and then go to prepare our rooms. I am weary."

The subdued Marcia ducked her head. "Yes, your highness."

Dex moved toward the door. "In the morning, if you feel up to it, and wish it, boss—we'll ride and I'll show you what the Pinon Ranch is made up of. Anything you want, Hop will be glad to get for you. Good night—and pleasant dreams."

She looked up at him and noted how his big, lithely poised figure filled the doorway. His eyes, as they met hers, were strange and brilliant and forceful. Her tone softened.

"Good night, Dexter Sublette."

III

Dex leaned against the wall of the bunkhouse, just inside the door. He was looking straight at Shorty. "I'll bet," he drawled, in excellent mimic—"I'll bet she'll be a string-necked old battle-axe, soured on the world and the male sex in particular. I'll bet she'll take an unholy delight in rawhiding us—"

Shorty Bartle squirmed painfully. "Quit it," he begged. "Quit it. I take it back. I take everything back. I was a liar by the clock. I was dumb—I didn't know what I was talking about. And for the Lord's sake, don't any of you jaspers ever breathe a word of what I spouted to her. Man—she shore is grand. Why, when she smiled at Dolf and me, I felt like I wanted to go out and knock a mountain down."

Wasatch Lane chuckled. "I can see where honest work on this spread is a thing of the past. Chuck, it will be up to you and me to do the laboring, while those two knot-heads will put in their time mooning around and putting sweet smelling hair oil on their stricken heads."

"You," said Shorty pointedly—"ain't seen them two ladies. Wait till you do."

"Oh, of course," mocked Wasatch. "Of course. You qualify as an expert. Both you jaspers are experts. Have you got it decided that this Marcia filly is a brunette yet?"

Shorty turned to Dex. "How about it, Dex? I claim Marcia is a—a titian, and Dolf, the dumb cluck—he claims she's a brunette."

"Of course she's a brunette," yelped Dolf. "You pig headed little wart, don't you know what a titian headed lady is like? She's got yellow hair, same as Dex. Ain't I right, Dex?"

Dex chuckled. "Right and wrong, Dolf. Marcia is a brunette, all right. But a titian is a red head, like Milly Duquesne."

"Yah," blurted Shorty. "You don't know so much, Dolf Andrews. You were right about the brunette part, but you didn't know no more about them titians than I did. You ain't so smart."

"Knew it," murmured Wasatch Lane—"knew it all

the time. I tell you, Dex—those two jaspers ain't going to be worth shucks around here from now on. They'll be putting in all their time trying to make their homely mugs good to look at so they can squire this Marcia critter."

"Not if I know it," grinned Dex, rolling a cigarette. "Listen here, you Shorty and Dolf. If your heads are getting full of romantic ideas, you knock 'em loose. You're not drawing wages to play Romeos. Work is going to be just as hard and steady as it ever was, maybe more so. I got a hunch this new boss of ours is a pretty shrewd little lady. She's going to demand results—and get them—if I have anything to say about it."

Shorty marched indignantly to his bunk. "Huh," he sniffed. "Listen to him will you. Him talking that way and he's worse than both Dolf and me put together. Yeah, go ahead and get red in the face. You ain't fooling me none. I watched the way you packed the princess into the house. You ain't had a drink for over a month that I know of, but you were drunk as a trout, just the same. Huh—you should preach."

A rumble of mirth came from Wasatch, Chuck and Dolf. Dex chuckled good-naturedly. "Have it your own way, Shorty. I guess I was kind of shaky. It was a brand new experience for me, and I felt clumsy as an ox. But just for your sass, in the morning you take the chuck wagon and high-tail it to town after the rest of the boss's trunks. How's the head, Chuck?"

"A lot better, Dex. I slept all afternoon. I'll be raring to go, tomorrow."

Dex sat on the edge of his bunk and pulled his boots off. His expression grew more serious. "I bumped into Alviso and three of his crowd on the way to town," he said. "Alviso stopped me and gave me a yarn of how Blitzen had gored up two of his bulls so bad he had to shoot them. I thought he was lying and I found it out a minute later when he went on to ask if there was any truth in the report circulating that a real princess was coming to live at this ranch."

Shorty reared up on one elbow. "I hope you told him where to go," he exploded.

Dex nodded. "I did. But you know what he did? He laid out there along the road so that he could see her as we were on the road home. And he had the nerve to lift his hat and smile at her."

Shorty bounced out of the blankets this time. "Did you crawl his frame?" he demanded hotly.

"It was no time or place to crawl anybody's frame," said Dex. "Not that I didn't feel like it, of course. I'll get that chance later."

Shorty was literally waltzing with wrath. "If that damned Spig ever looks at our princess when I'm around, him and me are going to the mat, proper. Why that low down whelp—I—I'll cut off his ears and choke him with 'em."

"Our princess," murmured Wasatch. "Listen to him, will you."

Shorty whirled on the old puncher. "You bet," he declaimed pugnaciously. "Our princess. That's just what she is. She's the grandest lady that ever hit these parts. And she's ours. She belongs to this spread. Where she's concerned I'm going to pack a chip on each shoulder and a gun in each hand. And the first wattle-necked buzzard that looks cross-eyed at her, I hang his hide up to dry."

Dex nodded, half seriously. "Nothing wrong with those sentiments, as long as you use a little judgment with 'em, Shorty. She's new to this country and there are a lot of rough edges here that we've got to protect her from. There's to be no fighting or brawling in front of her, unless, of course, it is absolutely necessary. She's a gentlewoman, come from gentle surrounding. We want to remember that. Any time it becomes necessary to teach some unruly jasper manners, we got to lead him out of sight before we work on him. We don't want her to get the idea that the men working for her are a bunch of salty necked wild-cats."

The sun was a good two hours high before Sonia Stephens appeared the following morning. By that time Shorty was well on his way to San Geronimo with the round-up wagon, bound for the several trunks which belonged to Sonia and with a long list of extra food supplies for Hop Lee's kitchen. Dolf and Wasatch, grimed with sweat and soot, were working at the portable forge, putting in shape a bundle of branding irons. Chuck was making some odd repairs about the corral fences, while Dex Sublette was busy cleaning up and making ready for use a small saddle he had resurrected from the store room.

For a time Sonia stood on the steps of the ranch-house, looking out over this new kingdom of hers. The house faced the west and, far out there against the morning jutted the crest of the Thunderheads. The air was warm, yet crisp and tingling with the vitality of elevation. The cottonwoods round about were whispering before the indolent push of a slight breeze. High on the swaying tip of a branch, a shimmering jewel of orange and black, an oriole poured liquid music from a golden throat. Lower down, just beyond one corner of the house, a family of purple finches twittered and sang. On a stone by the doorstep a gray backed lizard basked in the sunlight.

Sonia tipped back her head and filled her lungs to the utmost. This first real glimpse of her adopted country filled her with a heady exhilaration. Would this country, this mighty, tawny breasted country with its incredible distances, its limitless sweep of sun burnished sky, bring her the peace she had so long yearned for? She wondered.

Her shining eyes went over the corrals. She saw Dolf and Wasatch and Chuck. The music of industry was in the clang of Wasatch's hammer as he swung it on a branding iron. And then she saw Dex Sublette, swinging along, a saddle balanced on one shoulder. She caught his eye and waved impulsively. He dropped the saddle to the ground and shot up a long arm in acknowledging salute, then came up the low slope toward her.

"I am reminding you, Dexter Sublette," she said in

greeting—"that you promised to take me for a ride today. I am ready."

Dex's eyes were inscrutable as he looked at her. If she had been exquisite the day before, she was doubly so now. Slender and free limbed as a boy, she was, in riding breeches of expensive brown whip cord, tiny laced boots and cream silken blouse. The sun, pouring upon her bared head, brought out more strongly than ever the dark sheen of her hair. Dex felt almost dazed at the sheer, vibrant loveliness of her.

The intentness of his gaze caused her to color slightly. "You look," she said naïvely—"almost as though you were shocked. Do not women ever wear riding breeches in this country?"

"There are ways—and ways—of wearing them," drawled Dex slowly.

She frowned slightly. "You do not approve, then?"

Dex laughed softly. "Lord—yes! I'll tell a man I do. You're—well—kind of out of the ordinary, you know."

She still frowned. "I do not understand."

"You're a knock-out," said Dex. "A picture—almost too good to be true. I wonder if you realize how handsome you really are?"

Her frown broke into a slow smile. "I have had men tell me so before," she admitted. "But not quite in the manner you used. I like your way of complimenting me. It sounds sincere. But—are we going for that ride?"

Dex nodded. "I just over-hauled a saddle for you. But you better scare up a hat somewhere. If you don't,

52

you'll get your nose sun burned and sprout a crop of freckles."

She tossed her head. "I do not care. This sun—I cannot get enough of it. It is bright and pure and clean, and you've no idea how I crave such things."

"Fair enough," said Dex. "Come along. I want you to meet the rest of your crew."

As Dex swung along toward the corrals, she fell into step with him and there was a lightness, a girlishness about her now which made her seem incredibly young.

"You met Dolf last night," drawled Dex. "This old catamount is Wasatch Lane, the most confirmed woman hater in forty states. But his growl is worse than his bite."

Wasatch, meeting the clear beauty of her smile, squinted twinkling eyes. "Ma'am," he drawled, "that's a reputation I lose, right here and now. I've lived long and seen a lot, but I had to wait until I was an old man to meet the darling of my dreams. Seeing you, makes me realize that I didn't live in vain."

The clear music of her laughter seemed to brighten the morning. "You make me insufferably conceited," she said. "But that was very, very nice."

"It's a miracle," said Dex to Dolf. "I never thought that old badger would change his tune this way."

"I never saw a miracle before," retorted Wasatch imperturbably.

Sonia laughed again, but sobered as Chuck came up and she saw the bandage about his head. "You've been hurt," she exclaimed. "What—how did it happen?"

Dex threw a meaning look at Chuck, but Chuck did not need the warning. "A bronc tipped me off and my head came off second best in an argument with a rock," he answered cheerfully. "Mighty happy to meet you, ma'am. And I rise to say that Wasatch didn't even begin to paint the picture."

Sonia caught at Dex's arm. "Take me for that ride," she cried—"before I lose my head entirely."

He took her over to the cavvy corral. "Which pony am I to ride?" she asked.

"How'd that little liver and white pinto mare yonder suit you? A good little horse, sure footed and fairly fast, and not liable to fits of pitching. I'll put a rope on her."

Dex slithered over the fence, shook out a rope and made a quick, deft throw. He led the pinto over to the snubbing post. Dex looked back at Sonia. "Scramble in. I'll show you how to cinch on a hull. You may want to do it yourself, sometime."

Sonia climbed into the corral and Dex got the saddle, bridle and blankets.

"That saddle," said Sonia—"is small. It looks like it might have been made for a woman."

"It was," nodded Dex. "It belongs to Milly Duquesne. Before Bill Ladley left, Milly used to visit at the ranch a lot, and she kept this saddle out here to use if she felt like a ride."

"This—Milly Duquesne—who is she?"

"She lives in San Geronimo. Her daddy is a cattle buyer. Bill Ladley and Jack Duquesne were old friends. And Milly always called Ladley Uncle Bill."

"You know her—Milly Duquesne?"

Dex chuckled. "I shore do. I've known her ever since she was nothing but a scrawny legged kid. And if all the fights she and I had were put into one big fracas, it would make the last war look like a tea party. She's red headed, with a temper like a riled bob-cat. But a great girl. You'll have to meet Milly, because I know you'll like her."

While Sonia watched, Dex put the saddle on the little pinto. "Main thing is," he drawled—"is to get the saddle blanket smooth, keep the hull well forward and don't let the horse fool you by swelling up. They all try it and if you let 'em get away with it why the first thing you know, you'll have a slipping hull under you. You want to jab your knee into their tummy a couple of times and let 'em know who's boss. That will bring 'em down to natural size. Always work from the near side."

"Near side?"

"That's the left. We always speak of the left as the near side, the right as the off side. When you get the saddle in place to reach for the cinch—this way. This strap, the latigo, doubles through this ring—so. Then you make the tie, like that. Savvy?"

"I think so. I'll learn, with a little practice."

Dex slipped on the bridle, then turned. "All set. Up you go."

Again Sonia felt his hands grip her elbows and again she sensed the smooth flow of power in Dex's muscles as he tossed her lightly into the saddle. In spite of herself, a faint glow whipped through her cheeks. If Dex Sublette was finding her beauty a disturbing thing, she was finding him equally so. Dex was a different type of man than she had ever met before. There was a direct, engaging boyishness about him somehow, yet there was a stark, iron fibre discernible also, as though he possessed a sober experience far beyond his actual years. And every time she caught his face in profile she thought of an eagle, brilliant of eye, proud, fearless—bespeaking somehow a valiant, prideful heritage.

Dex roped and saddled a horse for himself, then opened the corral gate and waved Sonia out. Side by side they started down along Concho Creek. Soon they were out of the basin and beyond sight of the ranchhouse. And here they came across the first group of Pinon white-faces. Dex drew rein.

"Your cattle," he explained, building a cigarette. "And none better in the country. Get the brand on that yearling yonder. That is the Sawbuck brand—Bill Ladley's brand. But when you bought the ranch, you bought the brand. You can keep it or, if you'd rather, you can register a new brand, and we'll vent to it. But as it stands, the Sawbuck is a good brand, well known in these parts and mighty hard to blot. It will save a lot of time and expense if you keep it just as it is."

"I'm quite satisfied with it," said Sonia soberly. "There is much that I do not know about this business of running a ranch. In fact, I know nothing about it. I must rely entirely on your judgment."

"Maybe," drawled Dex, his eyes twinkling—
"Maybe I'll bunco you."

"Bunco? What is that?"

"Jip you. Steal from you."

She laughed lightly. "I am not afraid. Mr. Lockyear
wrote me that he strongly advised keeping you in
charge of the ranch. He said an awfully lot of very nice
things about you, Dexter Sublette. He said that if there
was anything you did not know about running a ranch,
it didn't matter anyhow."

"Now," chuckled Dex—"now it is my turn to get red
around the ears. I'll be getting all stuck up on myself.
But I'm glad he told you that. I'd hate like all get out
to have to leave the old spread—now."

Something in the way he used that last word made
Sonia look away. She pointed. "Tell me, why have
these cattle such ragged ears?"

Dex's chuckle grew to a delighted laugh. "I'll have
to tell the boys that one. We make those ears that way,
boss. It is, in a way, part of the sign of your ownership.
When we brand a slick, we earmark it, too. Pinon cattle
are earmarked swallowfork right, under slope left."

"You mean—you cut the ears like that?"

"That's right."

"But that is cruel," she flared.

"Not so much as you think. The cattle soon get over
it. And it is one of those necessary things."

"I don't see why."

Dex shrugged. "In this country there are plenty of
men with easy consciences concerning the cattle of

other people. Cattle—white-faces—look pretty much alike. An owner has to have some system of telling his stock from those of someone else. Branding and ear-marking have been found to be the best way of putting the sign of ownership on a cow."

"Perhaps you are right," she conceded. "But I still think it is cruel. I never want to witness any such operation."

Dex grinned. "Time you've been in this country for six months, you'll be just as tough as the rest of us."

They went on and all about her Sonia found objects of interest to exclaim over and ask questions about. Dex thought of an excited, eager child. It was easy to see that she had ridden a great deal. She had a true, well balanced seat in the saddle and she did not fight the rhythm of her horse. When they struck a long flat, she lifted the pinto to a run and the wind of progress, working at her hair, soon broke it loose and sent it cascading across her shoulders. Dex, loping along behind, smiled at the exuberance and joyous vitality of her.

Her quick eye picked up a slight movement in the grass beside the trail and she reined in swiftly and pointed. Dex, after a short chase, brought to her a tiny, quarter grown jack rabbit and in high delight she cuddled the little animal to her throat, petted it and cooed over it.

"Poor wee beastie," she crooned. "Its little heart is near bursting with fright. There, put it down again, where it can feel it is safe."

Dex obeyed, with the unspoken thought that if the

rabbit dodged the prairie hawks for the day it was doubtful if the coyotes of the night did not make quick work of it. But what Sonia did not know, would not hurt her, he reasoned. All too soon, no doubt, she would learn the ruthless cruelty of the stern hand of Nature.

As they went on, she stood high in her stirrups, her eyes fixed on the distant violet mass of the Thunder-heads. "Some time you must take me out there," she said. "I would like to explore the mystery of those mountains."

"When you feel up to a seventy mile ride, maybe we will go," said Dex dryly.

"Seventy miles!" she gasped. "Impossible."

"At least that far," Dex nodded.

"But they seem—only a little distance."

"I know. Distance in this country is always deceiving. I've seen the Thunderheads, after a storm, when they looked so close it seemed you could almost reach out and touch them. But they're a long way off. I'll show you, soon—just how far."

They came at length to the crest of the great, gray sage slope, which fell away so incredibly far to the mist shrouded depths of the Thunder River Canyon. Sonia gasped and was for a long time silent. She tried to measure the slope with her eye, but there was no unit of distance she was familiar with which could possibly serve. It was too great, too tremendous. And yet, great as was that part of the slope which she could discern, and unguessed the distance far below that was hidden in haze, beyond it all, at the very edge of the world it seemed, the Thunderheads reared their grim, terrific bulk against the sky.

Sonia drew a deep breath. "I—I understand," she said. "It makes me—almost—want to cry."

"We don't rate much, do we?" said Dex.

"There are men, in the country I wish to forget," she said in strange gravity—"men whom I wish could stand here and look at that. Perhaps it would teach them wisdom, make them realize of how little account their filthy lives are, how futile the thought that any mortal, whatever their fancied greatness and power, can permanently endure the force of the ages. I think this might expand their miserable souls."

Dex did not answer. These were her thoughts, spoken aloud, and he had no part in them.

She reined about suddenly. "Let us go back, Dexter Sublette. The picture is too terrific. It is something the human mind must absorb, slowly."

From the rim of the slope Dex took her back to a little dell he knew of along the creek, a moist shadowy little spot where the water ran crystal clear over burnished gravel, where there were moss covered rocks and still, green ferns. They dismounted and let the horses drink and Dex showed her the flicker of a frightened trout, as it raced from the shallows to the black pocket of depth. A water ouzel, swift and silent, flitted from rock to rock, and at times dipped fearlessly into the moist depths.

Sonia looked up at Dex with strange eyes. "Thank

you," she said simply. "I have my sense of proportion back, now."

They rode up out of the creek to the sear, rolling range once more. And Sonia was startled to see Dex rise in his stirrups, lean forward and bite back a muttered exclamation. She saw his jaw harden and steal out and the whimsical gray of his eyes turn to ice. Following his look she saw some half dozen mounted men riding directly toward them. In front, on a dashing bay, rode a man whose equipment glittered heavy silver in the sun. She recognized Don Diego Alviso.

At the moment Alviso had waved his followers to a halt, while he advanced alone, spurring the bay in showy, curvetting speed. Setting up the horse with hard, cruel strength, the Don swept off his sombrero with a flourish.

"Ah, Senor Sublette," he cried. "This is indeed a happy fortune, to meet you thus. And am I mistaken, or is this lady not the new owner of the Pinon Rancho?"

Don Diego Alviso's voice was slurring and musical, but Dex Sublette's reply had the harsh brittleness of two obsidian stones being clicked together.

"And if she is, Alviso, I fail to see how it concerns you in any way."

The Spaniard's black eyes narrowed just a trifle, but his smile persisted. "I would not be human if I failed to feel concern over the identity of a neighbor—such a charming neighbor. Surely you will honor me with an introduction?"

Dex hesitated, then shrugged. He turned stiffly.

"Miss Stephens, this is Don Diego Alviso. He runs the Lazy Cross outfit, out west of San Geronimo. I think I've already expressed my opinion of him to you."

Sonia, meeting Don Diego's eager, black eyes, inclined her head ever so slightly.

"This makes me very happy, Miss Stephens," said the Don, a trace of accent creeping into his words. "This has been a very lonely range. I trust I may see you again. You would honor me greatly if I had your permission to call upon you."

At this Dex stirred, a rippling surge of movement that started at his very heels. He leaned forward and his eyes turned hard and hostile.

"Miss Stephens is going to be very busy managing her ranch, Alviso," he growled.

The Don's retort was quick, telling and pointed. "Then you are not only the senorita's major domo, Senor Sublette—you are also her social advisor—yes?"

Sonia sensed the chill threat which lay in the air, sensed the animosity which lay like a live flame between these two men. And she was at a loss to understand it. True, this Don Diego was a trifle over-dressed and there was an oily suavity in his manner and words. Yet he was undeniably handsome in a dark and dashing way and his manners seemed impeccable.

And his retort to Dex could not have possibly been more cunningly calculated. It struck at the very heart of Sonia's imperious pride. After all, she was a princess. She could not immediately shake off the training and culture of years. She was still influenced by manner and appearance to some extent. And in the interchange of words between these two men, Dex Sublette had seemed almost boorish against the polished manner of the Don. It was only natural that her immediate partisanship lay with Dex. However, at the implied proprietorship his words had given, the woman in her flared.

"Indeed he is not, Don Diego," she answered quickly, her cheeks flaming. "Mr. Sublette is my foreman—his authority ends there. I will be glad to have you call at any time. I wish to be friendly with my neighbors."

Sonia missed the veiled sneer of triumph which glinted in the Don's eyes as he looked at Dex, but she did not miss the change in Sublette. The chill, hard set of his features remained the same, but a strange woodenness of expression made them still and unmoving, almost devoid of any life whatever, it seemed. His eyes remained utterly cold, but the glint in them seemed to veil itself and retreat. He shrugged and reined his horse a pace or two distant. He made one last remark, his voice even and dispassionate.

"Someday, Alviso—someday I'm going to kill you!"

Sonia was stunned, dumbfounded. That single short sentence had come out so quietly, so tersely that for a moment the full significance of it was lost on the girl. Then she caught her breath as she realized that this was not the threat of an angry man whose faculties, under the lash of rage, were momentarily beyond control. Instead, it was a death sentence, given much as though coming from the austere, somber authority of a judge's bench.

The effect on Don Diego was peculiar. His dark, sleek features convulsed and his eyes moiled with such feral lights as might be seen in the eyes of a cornered panther. Unconsciously he recoiled, reining his horse back a pace or two.

"If I should call up my men—" he began.

Dex Sublette cut him short with a cold, emotionless laugh. "If Miss Stephens wasn't here, you wouldn't have to call them up. I'd ride down to meet them and the smoke would be rolling. And you'd be dead before I had passed you. Now I'm telling you something. My patience is getting shorter all the time. If you want to keep your health, get off Pinon Range and keep off. Miss Stephens is new to this country and you might fool her for a time. But you can't fool me. I know you for just what you are. And so do the rest of the boys. Now, call your gang of mongrels and hit the trail."

The glances of the two men met and locked. The Don licked his over-red, somewhat sensuous lips. His eyes flickered and he looked away, to glance at Sonia, who was, by this time, a bewildered, indignant and just a little frightened spectator of the battle of wills between these two men. The Don forced a smile, and bowed.

"I shall not forget your kind invitation, Senorita," he said. "Adios."

He whirled his fretting mount and galloped back to

his men, giving them a terse order. They all rode off then, to the north and west. Dex, with emotionless face and eyes, watched them until they were out of sight. Then he relaxed slightly and shook the reins. "We better be moving if we expect to look over any more range this morning," he said gravely.

Now that the crisis was past, Sonia became typically feminine in the relief of her pent up nerves. She lit into Dex like a tornado.

"You were rude—you had no right—you embarrassed me terribly," she flared.

"Yes," agreed Dex, looking straight ahead.

"You were a savage—and the Don appeared to be a gentleman."

"Yes," agreed Dex once more. "That's right. He seemed to be."

This was not getting Sonia anywhere. "But I cannot imagine—I do not understand—" she stormed.

Dex favored her with a swift, fathomless glance. "Now you're getting down to cases. No—you don't understand. And until you do, suppose you withhold judgment. Let's ride."

Without giving her another chance to speak, Dex lifted his horse into a long, easy lope, leaving Sonia without any other recourse but to follow, fairly biting her lips with mortification.

IV

It was midday before Dex and Sonia got back to the Pinon ranchhouse. The morning ride had not been nearly as successful as Dex had hoped. He had intended that Sonia would have enjoyed it fully and, at the start, it appeared that such would be the case. But the meeting with Don Diego had spoiled everything; the magic of the earlier miles previous to the meeting as well as the ride home. He had warded off an incipient quarrel by refusing to argue the point with the furious Sonia and the natural outcome of it all had been a condition of rather strained, stilted formality.

There was a saddled horse standing at the corner of the corrals when Dex and Sonia rode up and a tall, lithe girl with hair like burnished copper, dressed in divided skirts, came down off the ranchhouse porch to meet them. She waved a friendly hand to Dex and hailed him. "Hi—compadre," she called. "How's things?"

Dex grinned as he dismounted. "Hello, Milly—out for a fight?"

Milly Duquesne laughed gaily. "Hardly—hardly. Not in a fighting mood today, Dex. I just wanted to be neighborly and hospitable. I wanted the chance of meeting Miss Stephens, of welcoming her to our country and to warn her against the devilish make-up of yourself, sir."

"Shore," drawled Dex. "That's nice of you, old brick-top. Miss Stephens, meet an old and valued friend, Milly Duquesne."

He had turned to help Sonia from the saddle, but she slipped to the ground unaided and stepped past him. Her nod was just a trifle stiff. "Charmed, I'm sure, Miss Duquesne. Won't you have lunch with me?"

"I expected to," smiled Milly with disarming frankness. "Hop Lee told me he was having my favorite dish, stew and dumplings. I can see that the stories are not a bit exaggerated."

"Stories?" Sonia looked puzzled.

"Dolf and Wasatch and Chuck have been filling my ears about you, my dear. Even Wasatch, who is about as impressionable as a rhinoceros, was raving. And they were all absolutely correct. You are—lovely."

There was a disarming frankness and honesty about Milly Duquesne which could not give offence. Sonia's attitude softened and her smile was genuine. "Everyone is very, very kind to me. Won't you come up to the house with me?"

"After a bit. You'll want to freshen up a bit, I suppose. Not that you show any signs of needing it. I wonder that my good friend Mr. Sublette is even partially sane after an all morning ride, with you. But while you are changing I want to habla with this long legged deceiver here."

Sonia laughed and nodded. "I'll be ready in fifteen minutes."

She swung past them and headed for the house. Milly looked after her. "She's got it, Dex," said the red head.

"Got what?"

"Class. A little stiff and formal, perhaps—but I think I can mellow her. Come on down to the corrals. I want to cry on your shoulder."

The change in Milly's tone surprised Dex. He turned and looked at her intently, realizing for the first time that behind her jocularity lay a strained intentness about her eyes and lips. And her cheeks, usually fresh and rosy, were a trifle pale.

Dex tucked his arm about her and started for the corrals, leading the two horses. "What's on your mind, old girl?" he drawled gently. "No bad news, I hope."

Milly nodded, biting her lips and trying to fight back a sudden rush of tears. "I—I think so, Dex," she murmured brokenly. "I haven't heard a word from Tommy for nearly two months. I used to hear every week. I don't see why he and Dad ever got such a fool idea of starting a ranch up down in the Argentine. Tommy, if you stop to think, has been gone nearly eight months, now, looking things over. And that is wild country, Dex—and I—I'm afraid—afraid—" A sob choked her and she let her fair head drop on Dex's shoulder.

Dex's arm tightened about her. He patted her shoulder. "Here—here," he scolded gently. "None of that—none of that. Don't you get to worrying about that boy Tommy. He's not the kind to let anything get him down. There can be lots of reasons why you haven't heard from him lately. The mail might be held up—he might be on his way home—oh, a lot of things of that sort. Give the boy a chance. He'll be home and marrying you, one of these days. But if he keeps on worrying you much longer, I'll go down there and hunt him up and whale hell out of him."

The confidence in Dex's words was heartening to Milly and presently she dried her tears, pecked a kiss against his cheek and drew away. "He better be getting home," she said with a tremulous smile—"or I'll forget him entirely and enter the lists after your handsome scalp, my good friend. But no fooling—you've made me feel a lot better, Dex old boy. You always were an optimistic cuss. Now let's see if we can't think up something to fight about."

Dex laughed. "Nothing doing. I had one squabble with a lady already today, and I'm not hankering for another."

"Dex Sublette! Did you quarrel with that exquisite little creature—that new boss of yours?"

"Um. I reckon you might call it a quarrel. I reckon she was ready to scratch my eyes out for a while."

"What did you fight about?"

"I tried to tell her the moon was made of green cheese. She wouldn't believe me."

Milly made a face at him. "You wouldn't let your own grandmother in on a secret. All right for you. But the time will come when I'll have a secret, and then I'll let you hanker. I hope you didn't make a chump of yourself in front of your boss."

Dex grinned wryly. "Go on—beat it. Hike for the house, before I dust your britches with a quirt. I'm in one of my sulky spells."

Milly laughed. "That's a sure sign. But I don't blame you a bit, old timer. If I was a man I'd be in love with her myself."

"You," said Dex severely—"are shore inviting that licking."

Milly waved, laughed again and hurried up to the house. And Dex's face, as he began unsaddling, grew thoughtful and bleak.

It did not take the breezy, genuine Milly Duquesne long to break down most of the barrier of Sonia's reserve. Milly's wit was quick, her perceptions keen. She was swift to see what Dex had missed, and that was an almost breathless eagerness on the part of Sonia to be absorbed in this western scheme of things. It was as though she wanted to entirely bury her older self and all it represented and to take on new character.

"She's been hurt—bad," mused Milly—"Somewhere along the back trail she has taken her whipping—and she wants to forget it, entirely. That revolution, no doubt—and perhaps a man. Poor youngster. She's just a little bewildered and scared. She has a tough job on her hands, trying to shuck the training and teaching of years. I'll do my best for her."

Milly's best was a lot. In casual, slangy, breezy discourse, she led Sonia into a bright, unaffected mood and long before the lunch was over with, the two of them were chatting and laughing as though they had known each other for years. And not until Milly mentioned Dex Sublette, did Sonia's attitude change.

"I am not sure that I altogether approve of Dexter Sublette in his present position," said Sonia, frowning slightly. "Up until this morning—yes. And now I am not so sure."

Milly played her cards very carefully. "Where men are concerned, I pride myself in being very hard to please," she said. "Yet, I don't mind saying that I think Dex is the most completely perfect man I have ever known. Almost too perfect," she added with a disarming smile. "That is the reason he and I have such a time getting along. We are always squabbling."

"What do you mean by the word—perfect?" asked Sonia with a casual disinterest which did not fool Milly in the slightest. Milly's blue eyes twinkled.

"In the first place, his code of honor is beyond reproach. What Dex should have been is a knight of the olden days. Then he could have donned his armor and gone out to slay all the dragons ever thought of. He's so darned honest he's almost offensive. He wouldn't lie if it would save his best friend from being hung. Which is one of the reasons I fight with him so much. He tells me the absolute truth about myself, and it isn't always complimentary. And if any woman is ever lucky enough to wring a real compliment from him, you can bet he means it. He isn't saying it just to be polite."

"I think," decided Sonia—"I shall tell you what happened this morning."

"You darling!" exclaimed Milly. "I'm dying to know. I knew that something was wrong—I can read old Dex like a book. But when I asked him he shut up like a clam."

Sonia told of the meeting with Don Diego and his men. She told of the interplay of words between the two men. "And," she ended—"Dexter Sublette told the Don that some day he would—kill him. I could see no perfection in that."

"Dex," said Milly drily—"was absolutely right. Don Diego Alviso isn't fit to even look at you, my dear. Yes, check up another credit to Dex."

"But," protested Sonia—"he had no right to decide who should call on me and who should not. That is a privilege I reserve for myself."

"I'm going to tell you something about Don Diego Alviso," declared Milly. "And then I'll leave it to you to decide whether you want him to call on you. I don't believe you want him now, except as a gesture to show Dex his place. Am I right?"

The eyes of the two girls met. Sonia colored slightly, then nodded. "You are very discerning," she murmured. "But what about Don Diego Alviso?"

"The best thing that can be said of him is that quite a few people around here believe that the Don throws an easy rope and a long one. Which means, in plain English that he isn't always too particular whose stock he puts his branding iron on. In other words that he qualifies very well as a cattle thief. As for the worst of him—well—there was a girl. Alberta Menlo would never have taken any prizes for brains, but she was a right decent sort of a little fool. Her folks were fine people. They owned the Diamond M ranch, which is out the other side of Alviso's spread. The Don—he has a weakness for women—turned that child's head. She ran away with him. The last word was that she had died in some kind of a joint down across the Border—in Mexico. It broke her parents all to pieces. They sold their ranch and moved East.

"A thing of that sort is just what would send Dex Sublette on the war-path. That is why Dex despises Don Diego so—that is why he said he would some day kill him. And that," Milly ended, a little fiercely—"is why I hope he does."

A deep, inscrutable light had come into Sonia's eyes. "I think," she said softly—"I think I owe Dexter Sublette an apology."

Milly stayed all afternoon, but declined Sonia's invitation to spend the night at the ranch. "I've got to get back to town," said Milly. "I've got a big baby of a Dad to look after. And," she added, a little wistfully—"I've been expecting a letter. Maybe it came in on the afternoon train."

That night, after supper, Hop Lee came shuffling into the bunkhouse. "Missy Boss wants see you, Boss Dex," he chattered.

Dex stood up slowly. "Go on, you lucky stiff," growled Shorty. "Why wasn't I born lucky enough to be foreman of a spread with a princess for boss? Some jaspers have all the luck in this danged old world."

Dex smiled gravely. "She probably wants to give me hell for something. If I come back all broken and wounded, I hope you fellows will take care of me."

"Gwan," blurted Shorty, throwing a deck of cards

down on the bunkhouse table. "How about a little stud, gentlemen—to take our minds off our troubles? All right, Hop—you can sit in, too. But watch yourself, you saffron colored tree toad. You come up with too many aces and your ancestors in dear old China will never hear from you again."

Hop grinned delightedly and drew up a chair.

Dex walked up to the ranchhouse slowly. The twilight was full and rich. As the reflection of the sunset faded, the purple shadows came massing, growing magically where none had been before. Against the last fading blaze of the western sky, the Thunderheads stood black and cold and austere. The moon was already above the eastern horizon, pale and ghostly, but increasing in its radiance as the shadows crept higher and higher.

At one end of the porch, in their industry at cleaning house the day before, Dolf and Shorty had hung an old canvas hammock they had resurrected from somewhere. In this, dressed in a soft white frock, Sonia was curled.

"Evening," said Dex gravely. "Nice night."

She laughed—softly. "How long have you been thinking up that stupendous speech, Mr. Dexter Sublette?"

"I've got to watch what I say," Dex said pointedly. "The last time I opened my mouth in front of you I got into trouble."

"I know," she nodded. "And I'm sorry. That is why I sent for you. I wish to apologize for—well, the way I acted today. Milly, she's a lovely girl—told me many things, today. She told me—about Don Diego Alviso. And you have my authority, Dexter Sublette, to order that beast off this ranch forever, the next time you see him."

"Keno!" exclaimed Dex. "That means a lot, Boss—to have you say that. Always remember—anything the boys or I may do, it is always for your own good, no matter how it may seem or sound at the time. You belong to the Pinon Ranch, you know. Why Shorty is already calling you 'our princess'."

The music of her laugh sounded again. "I like that, really. It makes me feel secure. You may smoke if you like."

Dex pulled up a chair, then built a smoke.

She did not seem real as she sat there. Her dress was some white, soft, sheening thing and the increasing brilliance of the moon had begun to pick up facets of light in the dark crown of her hair. Her face was a shadowy oval, mysterious and intriguing.

"Tell me," asked Dex, after a considerable silence. "Do you think you are going to like this country?"

"I'm sure," she exclaimed quickly. "I think there must be a strain of savage in me somewhere. At any rate, even though it frightens me, the vastness, the elemental greatness of it all, grips me. I love it. Away back in the centuries, my ancestors must have ridden shaggy ponies over the limitless steppes of Siberia and camped under the icy crests of unnamed mountains. There must be Tartar blood in me somewhere. For here—I am content. And I thought I never would be again, at one time. Look—look out there at the Thunderheads. What is there to say that would mean anything?"

"Only, that they never let you down," drawled Dex.

They were quiet again. Dex cleared his throat. "I don't know whether Lockyear gave you the full picture of this ranch. You saw some of it today, but here are some figures which might interest you. The latest tally promises around two thousand head of stock. Your range runs east and west about four miles each way with the ranch buildings as a center. Due south it runs a good ten miles and about seven to the north. It's a good spread, any way you look at it. You made no business mistake in buying. You'll have a prime lot of shipping beef ready for the market next spring. Anyway you look at it, I'd say you were sitting pretty."

"You make it sound almost as though I were ruling—" She broke off abruptly, jumped to her feet and walked over to the porch rail, staring out across the shimmering night. "No," she murmured, as though to herself—"not that. I want to forget all such things."

Dex shifted restlessly in his chair. She was trim and graceful, like a reed swaying before the wind. Dex got up and stood beside her, and he was thinking that at this same hour on the previous evening she had been asleep, within the circle of his arm. And with this thought came an unruly tide of emotion breaking loose within him.

He looked down at her dark head, so close to his shoulder and his eyes grew hungry and wistful. Quite suddenly he understood that aching emptiness within him. He knew now that it had always been there, waiting through the years for the love of a woman like this to fill it. He wanted to catch her up to him, to crush her in his arms. He began to tremble, in the grip of a blinding palsy of emotion.

It seemed that the very intensity of this strange storm which was shaking him, communicated itself to Sonia. She looked up at him and her eyes were pools of mystery. Her lips were slightly parted.

"Sonia!" whispered Dex hoarsely. "Where have you been through all these years. I've seen you in the flames of a thousand campfires, in the stars, in the sunshine and the driving storm. And now I find you here—not a dream, but a reality. I want you—for I've loved you forever!"

She was still as a dew kissed flower, as fragrant—as mysterious and with the same haunting loveliness. One hand fluttered to her throat. It seem that she leaned toward him—yet it might have been a trick of that treacherous moonlight. Yet her face lifted until the crimson magic of her lips was so close—so close—Dex kissed her.

In a flash she was away from him, on the opposite side of the hammock, where she faced him, head up, hands clenched—her eyes flaming.

"So!" Her voice was as cold and cutting as the edge of honed steel. "You would presume on the thought that I am 'your princess', eh? That is twice today you have known the touch of a woman's lips. Miss

Duquesne's this morning—and now—mine. You like them perhaps. And you do it so casually. Pfaugh!"

She scrubbed her lips furiously with the back of one small hand, as though to remove something unclean. She stamped her foot. "The shame of it," she choked, half sobbing. "Mawkish love making under the moon—petting—as I have heard you Americans call it. And I—one of royal blood—caressed by—by—"

"One who is your equal, lady," broke in Dex harshly. He was standing very straight and tall, his face a set mask, his eyes chill and pain wracked. "I too have royal blood—the blood of men who helped to tame a wilderness—the blood of real achievement. My ancestors tackled a stern land with their bare hands and made it good. Their bones mark the outposts of a great nation's frontiers. My grandfather was William Lewis Sublette, who traveled the fur trails across the deserts and past the last frozen mountain range. My ancestors lived for an ideal—and died for it. They knew true nobility."

She did not answer. She was crying.

Dex went on, jerkily. "This—tonight—forget it. Blame it on the moon. I'm begging your pardon. It won't happen again—ever. You've my word on that—and I'm particular about keeping my word. If I've hurt you—then you've had more than your money's worth. You've heard words tonight I never spoke before—words I never expected to speak—for I never hoped that an ideal would ever be more than just—an ideal. But those words were worthy and, though it may seem strange to you—I meant every one of them. Good night."

He put one hand on the porch rail, vaulted to the ground and strode quickly away into the moon haze.

V

Two weeks went by. They might have been the longest and most torture filled weeks of Dexter Sublette's entire existence, had he not subdued the agony of spirit in slave driving physical action and work. He had ordered the calf round-up and inside of two days had Wasatch and Shorty and Dolf and Chuck shaking their heads in stubborn wonder. Overnight, so it seemed to them, Dex had become another individual—a man with a single purpose of work, work, work. Not that he asked more of the others than he was willing to give himself. He did as much as any two of the others, and every night found the outfit half drugged with exhaustion.

Dex's face had become a mask, hard and bitter, with lines of repression carved deep about his lips. His eyes were stoic, unreadable. When he spoke, which was seldom, his orders were terse, sure and full of chill authority.

"Crazy," growled Shorty one night, when Dex was not present in the bunkhouse. "Crazy as a sheep-herder. What in hell has bit him, anyhow?"

Wasatch waggled his grizzled thatch wisely. "The boy is sick," he opined.

"Sick!" snorted Shorty. "Shore I'd hate to see him in full health again. For a sick man he can do more than any hombre I ever laid eyes on before. From trying to keep half way in his dust I'm plumb wore out, right down to a dizzy frazzle. I've aged ten years in the last two weeks. A blind man could count my ribs. I wouldn't work this hard for any other man under the sun except old Dex. But if he don't slow up he's going to have my death laid at his door."

"Stay with it," grinned Wasatch. "Times will get better."

Up in the big house, Sonia Stephens was beginning to have her first qualms about the wisdom of this venture of hers into the western cattle country. For she was much alone, now. She had time for thinking—too much thinking. The days moved on with a tempo which never changed and Sonia, who was naturally of a vigorous, restless disposition, began to chafe at the inaction. Her first fears of a recurrence of personalities on the part of Dex Sublette proved groundless. She saw him but a few times during those two weeks, and never alone. If he had anything about the ranch to discuss with her, he always managed to have Marcia present at the time, and his attitude was one of polite, restrained, impersonal business. The engaging boyishness of him was gone now, and his face seemed haggard from fatigue. His eyes looked at her, through her, past her.

When the first keen edge of her resentment had worn off, Sonia knew a qualm of pity every time she glimpsed that set, cold haggardness of Dex's face. After all, had the blame been all his? She knew in her heart that she had welcomed that kiss—that she had leaned toward him, that the mystery of the moon drenched night had carried her away, just as it had him. Her conscience kept telling her that she had been unfair. She was furious with herself—furious with him.

She, who had been reared in a world where romance—where love, caresses—were the outcome of long and sedately consummated courtship, had been kissed by a splendid, tawny haired savage, whom she had known but little longer than a day. Worse—at the time she had welcomed it. It was enough to frighten anyone, and if her reaction had been angry and contemptuous, it had been in self-defense.

Yet she could not disguise from herself the fact that Dex Sublette's abrupt about face in manner had left her with a distinct sense of loss. It was as though she had glimpsed the white glow of a beautiful flame and then seen it pinched out forever. And that hurt, whether she liked it or not.

She tried to get away from herself by going on long rides. And each time she did, the puncher who saddled her pony saddled one for himself. She was not permitted to ride alone. The first time this had happened she knew a spark of annoyance.

"You need not ride with me," she told Dolf, who had drawn the assignment. "I do not wish to take you from your work."

"Sublette's orders, ma'am," shrugged Dolf.

"Then I will see him, if you please."

Dolf went after Dex, who came up, dusty and grimed from work over the branding fire. "I am no child," said Sonia stiffly. "This is ridiculous that I must have a guardian every time I wish to go for a ride."

"Sorry," answered Dex evenly. "But Dolf will go with you."

Sonia stamped her foot. "But I do not wish it. Have I no authority on my own ranch?"

"You have all the authority except on this one thing, ma'am. It is for your own good. As long as I am foreman here, it will have to be that way."

He was looking at her sternly. She acquiesced abruptly. "Very well, if you think it best."

But if she expected any sign of reacting warmth from Dex by this concession, she was doomed to disappointment. Dex merely nodded, turned and stalked away. The man had become as adamant as stone. And Sonia got little pleasure out of that ride.

Sonia would not have been human had she remained unaffected by the pointed manner in which Dex Sublette avoided her, except when business absolutely demanded that he see her. Nor could she be unaffected by the way his eyes looked upon her with such impersonal gravity. This man who had been so vital, so full of charm and interest had moved away from her to a distance and beyond a barrier of reserve which she could neither travel nor cross. And the condition stung her to calculated effort. She did her best to get Dex alone, to bring him even part way back without bending her knee too for her own self-respect. But though she laid her traps with cunning, Dex avoided them with even greater cunning.

One evening, when Dex was reporting a phase of work to her, when he stood bare-headed before her, hat in hand, Sonia turned to Marcia. "It is chill, Marcia. Fetch me a wrap."

As Marcia left the room, Sonia faced Dex determinedly, her eyes on the drawn set of his face. Her tone softened. "You are working too hard. Is it necessary to wear yourself out so, for the interests of another?"

"I was raised on hard work," answered Dex evenly. "And the work has to be done. Now about those yearlings I was speaking of—"

Sonia made an impatient gesture. "Bother the cattle," she exploded. "Is there nothing about this ranch but cattle—cattle—cattle? Can there be no conversation except on business—the ranch—and then more cattle? There was one—night—when—"

"I have decided that night never existed," broke in Dex quietly. "And if you do not care to hear about those yearlings—"

"No, I don't," cried Sonia in baffled annoyance.

"Very well," drawled Dex, turning away. "Good evening, ma'am."

When Marcia got back with the wrap, Sonia was alone and pacing the room in sparkling eyed fury. And she did not want the wrap after all. She tossed it aside impatiently.

The final morning of the calf branding saw Sonia, dressed in her riding togs, marching determinedly down into the big meadow, her black head gleaming in the sunlight, her little dove gray Stetson hat swinging in one hand by the chin thong. Down where the cattle were, all was bedlam, dirt and dust—with the air full of the stench of scorched hide and hair.

The work was moving smoothly. Calf after calf was roped and dragged up to the branding fire—bucking, bawling and struggling on the ends of the taut ropes. Here the luckless little beasts were flipped and held, while the branding irons smoked against their flanks and keen knives in practiced hands flashed through the ear-marking cuts.

There was something about it, despite the grime and noise and smell, which thrilled Sonia. There was an elemental vitality about it somehow. Her eyes followed Dex. Even at this back-breaking toil there was a lithe, poised sureness about his every movement and every time he flipped a bawling, struggling little white-face she could see the magnificent muscles of his back and shoulders coil and glide beneath his sweat drenched shirt.

Abruptly Dex saw her and he came over to her swiftly. Sonia's pulses fluttered strangely and her elfin under lip began to pout in the beginnings of a smile. But she was rudely jarred by Dex's words.

"You shouldn't be down here—afoot," he told her harshly. "Those cows get pretty badly worked up when we rope their calves. One of them may go on the warpath any minute. Go on back to the corrals and get your pony."

Sonia stiffened, cut by the harsh abruptness of him. "You are working on foot," she said.

"That is different," he said curtly. "I know what to expect. If you want to watch this work, go get a horse."

"I'm sorry," she flared. "But I am not yet expert enough to catch and saddle my own pony."

Dex hesitated, then shrugged. He turned and started for the corrals. "I'll saddle your bronc for you."

When he turned over the ready mount for her, he started back to the herd. "You'll be able to watch in safety, now."

"But I am not going to watch," she said. "I am going for a ride."

Dex turned and looked at her. "We're nearly done with this job. If I can keep all the boys at it, we'll be done by tonight. Can't you put that ride off until tomorrow?"

"I will ride alone."

"You will not. Wait here. I'll send Chuck to go with you."

Sonia lost her temper completely, then. "I am tired of being handled like a child," she cried. "This situation is unbearable."

"Whether you like it or not, you'll have to put up with it," stated Dex grimly. "I'm responsible for your safety."

"But Milly Duquesne rides alone, and—"

"Milly was born and bred to this country. She can take care of herself," cut in Dex.

Sonia chose to misread the inference in Dex's words. "And I am not, I suppose," she flamed furiously. "I'll show you—"

She swung into the saddle. Dex jumped and caught her bridle rein. And at that moment, swinging down from above the ranchhouse came a rider on a curvetting bay gelding. It was Don Diego Alviso.

The Don was alone and he came straight up to them. His sombrero came off with a flourish and his swarthy face broke into a white toothed smile.

"Ah, Senorita—is it that fortune favors me this day? Is it that I find you about to start upon a ride across the range, or into San Geronimo, perhaps? Should you allow me to accompany you, then indeed would you give me a great happiness."

Sonia had imagined, after listening to Milly Duquesne's scathing indictment of Don Diego, that her next meeting with the man would leave her filled with repulsion and disgust. Had her present mood been one of normal serenity, no doubt this would have been true. But Sonia was not her usual self at this moment. She was angry—furiously angry with Dexter Sublette. She felt that she had gone out of her way, indeed made almost open advances in her effort to break through the unyielding armor he had clothed himself in. And she had gotten nowhere. In her present anger she was swayed with the sudden wish to hurt Dex, to wound him. And here, right before her was the means. Therefore she returned the Don's smile and inclined her head.

"I see no reason why you should not accompany me,

Don Diego. I will be delighted to have you."

The Don swung his mount closer, his eyes gleaming with triumph. "You honor me greatly, senorita. And we shall ride—where?"

"Miss Stephens is riding nowhere with you, Alviso," broke in Dex's voice, harsh and level. "But you—you're about due to travel—fast."

"I believe," said Sonia, her voice dangerously cool—"that I said I would ride with Don Diego. Perhaps you failed to hear me, Mr. Sublette."

"I heard you. But that sort of talk is foolish. You are not going."

Sonia's anger broke all bounds. "You will kindly attend to your own affairs, Dexter Sublette," she stormed. "You forget who I am."

"Wrong," gritted Dex. "You forget who he is."

Sonia's answer was to lift her quirt and bring it down across the flank of her pinto. The little mare leaped and reared, but could not break free of the steely grip Dex had on the reins.

Sonia was fairly shaking with the anger which tore her. She lifted the quirt again. "Will you loose that rein?" Her voice was little more than a thick, choked whisper. Her face had gone deathly pale and tiny spots of crimson glowed high on her cheeks.

"No," said Dex. "I won't let go of the rein."

With a little, whimpering cry she struck, once—twice—three times. Fair across Dex's face and chest and bare, bronzed throat the leather bit, and beneath its supple cruelty there sprang into being livid, fiery welts.

The third blow bruised his lips and a trickle of blood showed.

Dex did not cringe nor flinch nor say a word. He merely looked at her and there was something in his eyes which scorched the fury from Sonia and brought her suddenly to a remorseful, humped, weeping little bundle. She tried to speak, to cry out for his forgiveness, but the sobs in her throat choked back all utterance.

Then Dex dropped her rein and stepped past her. His purpose was in his eyes. Dex was unarmed, having left his gun on his saddle, down at the branding work. And Don Diego Alviso, reading aright the expression of this man stalking steadily toward him, started backing the bay gelding slowly away, while he dropped a hand to one of his ivory butted guns.

"Use caution," snarled the Don. "You are asking for death, senor!"

Dex laughed as he leaped. The Don jerked out the gun and fired at point-blank range. But Dex's sudden leap had startled the bay gelding and it was rearing and whirling even as the heavy bellow of the gun rolled. The lead flew high and wild. And before the Don could thumb another shot, Dex had him, jerking him from the saddle.

Dex spun him into the clear and hit him, a pile-driving smash that made a mess of Alviso's mouth and nose. It knocked him flat on the ground, where he lay immobile for a moment, dazed and bleeding. Dex snatched those ivory butted guns and flung them aside. Then he dragged the Don to his feet and started in on him with both fists. Three times he knocked the Spaniard down and three times he dragged him to his feet. But after the fourth crushing knockdown the Spaniard stayed there, senseless and limp.

Sound of that gunshot had brought Wasatch and Dolf, Shorty and Chuck, spurring up from the branding meadow. It took them but a moment to understand.

"When he comes out of it," grated Dex harshly— "head him for his own range. And tell him that the order is out to shoot him on sight if he ever puts foot on Pinon range again."

Dex started then, for the bunkhouse. "Who quirted you, Dex?" growled Shorty.

Dex did not answer. Shorty looked at Sonia and his pugnacious features hardened. "I thought," he said pointedly—"that a princess was too big for a stunt like that."

"Shut up!" growled Wasatch. "Help me with this skunk."

They dragged Don Diego to his feet, shook him until some of his addled senses came back, then thrust him toward the bay.

"You're lucky, greaser," Wasatch bit out coldly. "Dex is too generous with a pole-cat like you. Had I my way I'd kill you, right here and now. Next time you do get it, savvy? The next time it is hot lead. You ever show on this range again and any of us fellows shoot on sight. Remember that, if you want to live. Now—git!"

Wasatch punctuated this last order with a well placed kick which nearly upset the Don again. But the latter was too broken, too crushed of flesh and spirit to even react to his indignity. He fumbled wildly for the reins and crawled slowly into the saddle. Then he rode away at a, furious pace, lurching from side to side as he fought to regain his shattered equilibrium.

Sonia sat stunned and bewildered by the terrific, smashing ruthless manner in which Dex Sublette had virtually annihilated Alviso with his bare hands. And she had tried, her glance humble, tear-washed and beseeching, to catch Dex's eye as he headed for the bunkhouse. But he passed her as though she had ceased to exist.

Now, her knees trembling so she could hardly stand, she slipped from her saddle and turned to the four riders, willing to be comforted by anyone in this pit of misery which had engulfed her. It was Wasatch who took the rein of her pinto, but there was no comfort in his grim old features. Dolf and Shorty and Chuck rode away toward the bunkhouse. Sonia found herself alone, so thoroughly and pointedly alone that she felt her heart would break. She went slowly, haltingly up to the ranchhouse, through sunlight which had no color or warmth whatever.

VI

Shorty and Dolf and Chuck entered the bunkhouse to find Dex Sublette lying flat on his back on his bunk, staring at the ceiling. They looked at the welts on his face and throat, welts that stood out in purplish ugliness now. They cursed softly and began packing their war-bags. Dex turned his head, saw what they were doing, and snapped upright.

"And what in blazes do you think you're going to do?" he demanded.

"Quit," said Shorty stoutly. "I reckon you'll be traveling pretty soon and Dolf and Chuck and me figure to trail along. Wasatch will be here in a minute and he's ready to go with us. She may be a princess and all that, but she shore can't quirt a pal of ours and get away with it. Not when he's doing something for her own good."

The brittle, expressionless bleakness in Dex's eyes softened slightly. "You damned lunk-headed chumps," he growled. "Put those war-bags away and get out at the branding. Nobody is quitting around this spread—not for a while, anyhow. We're not going to pull out and leave Miss Stephens and Marcia here alone. You ought to know that. Anyhow, she was plumb mad and didn't understand—then. I think she does, now. Anyway, this scrap is between her and me. I've known the burn of hot lead more than once. I reckon a little quirting won't keep me down. So get along out and finish up with those calves. Hike!"

The three punchers hesitated, looked first at Dex and then at each other, swore, shoved their war-bags aside and went out. And hardly had they gone than Marcia hurried in, round eyed, clucking to herself in concern. At sight of Dex's face she exclaimed in pity and crossed resolutely to him.

"For shame," she murmured—"for shame. Your poor face."

Dex tried to object, but Marcia was resolute. She brought water, soaked cloths and laid cooling compresses on the welts. And while she worked, she talked.

"You must not be too hard with her, Mr. Dex. After all she is only a child, with a great deal to learn about life—and other things. Right now she is up in her room, crying her eyes out."

Dex nodded. "I'll try and understand. Thanks a lot, Marcia."

When the cool compresses had taken some of the vicious swelling out of the welts, she smeared them gently with a healing ointment, gathered up her stuff and left. Alone with his thoughts, Dex tried hard to get Sonia's viewpoint. The natural pride of him, always a strong and living flame, was stung to the quick. Sonia had quirted him, almost viciously, under the very eyes of Don Diego Alviso. True, Alviso had had little time in which to gloat before the power of Dex's fury had rolled over him like a tidal wave. But he had seen it, just the same, and the ignominy of it made Dex's very soul writhe.

Another thing that hurt had been Sonia's readiness to ride with the Don. She had virtually shuddered with aversion that night when she had called Alviso a beast and had told Dex that he had her permission to order Alviso off Pinon range forever, at the next opportunity. Yet, when Alviso did show up, she had been ready to ride with him.

Of course she had been furious at that moment. Being human, she could not be blamed for losing her sense of judgment to some degree. Yet, even so, there would be limits of folly to which such anger might lead her. Dex could not figure it out.

He shook his head a little wearily, got to his feet and surveyed his features in the battered old looking glass above Shorty's bunk. At sight of the welts, still savage and cruel looking in spite of Marcia's treatment, his lips pulled into a hard, straight line and his eyes chilled anew. It was going to be hard—forgetting.

Dex felt incredibly weary. For weeks now he had been drawn to a taut, harsh edge. While that tension had endured he had been virtually unconscious of fatigue. He had been riding on his nerve. In a way, the emotional explosion he had known when he went after Don Diego, had been a benefit to him. He had gotten a lot of simmering emotional strain out of his system. It was as though his feelings had been damned tightly. Now the flood gates had been opened and he felt dry and spent, but queerly relieved. Yet he was tired— tired—

He started back for his bunk, but at that moment there came to his ears, faint with distance, the protesting bawl of still another calf which felt the sear of the branding iron. There was still work to be done. He flexed his arms, drew a deep breath and went on out to his toil.

The Pinon outfit slept late. The grind of the calf

roundup done, the immediate rush of work was over with. The riders lolled about the bunkhouse, shaving, cleaning up, getting in a few necessary needle and thread repairs on clothes that had taken a beating.

A new quietude had come over the outfit. The subject of those welts on Dex's face was scrupulously avoided, but the constant visual reminder of them had a subduing effect on the riders. Even the garrulous, irrepressible Shorty had little to say. And Dex, not fooled a bit by the unaccustomed silence, knew that something had to be done to put the mind of the outfit on other things.

"We're not just writing off the loss of that saddle stock," he said. "It is even more important than locating the horses, to see if we can get a lead on who stole them, if possible. Thinking it over, it couldn't very well have been Alviso. It was Sawtelle, or some other crowd new to us. I'm guessing it was Sawtelle. The whole play was too well figured out to be the work of a strange crowd. What we've got to do is locate the crossing of Thunder River Canyon. For Sawtelle is liable to come again. And if he does, we've got to know the trails, if we're to stand any chance of catching him. So—I'm taking Shorty and Dolf and hitting for the canyon again. We'll take grub and blankets with us and may be gone four or five days."

"Can you think of any good reason for leaving Chuck and me behind?" drawled Wasatch. "I can't."

"Best reason in the world," nodded Dex, jerking his head toward the ranchhouse. "With Alviso running loose and as full of poison as he's going to be from now on—somebody has *always* got to be on hand—here."

Wasatch nodded, but looked sourly at Shorty. "You may bump into Sawtelle or some of that wild outlaw crowd," he growled. "If you do, you want a first class fightin' man along, not a hairbrained runt like that."

"Is that so?" yelped Shorty. "Why you fuzzy eared old relic, you never saw the day you could hold a candle to me, when it came to a fight. I'm the fightenest hombre in four states. Dex is using his head in picking me. I'll tell a man."

Dex smiled gravely. "You go out and rope up a pack horse, Shorty. I think that Oregon claybank mare is the one we want. Dolf, you go up to the big house and have Hop make up a pack of grub for us. I'll make up a couple of soogan rolls. Fly to it. We're leaving right away."

Shorty and Dolf went out. Dex looked at Wasatch.

"I'm leaving you and Chuck here because you're both older and more level headed than Shorty or Dolf. Miss Stephens will listen to you, Wasatch. You'll be able to do more with her, should she get some sudden idea—and your job is a damn sight more important than what we're going to do."

Wasatch nodded. "Fair enough," he growled. "But any time you're ridin' where the smoke might roll, I kinda like to be handy to you, kid."

Dex put his hand on Wasatch's shoulder and squeezed. "I know," he said softly. "And you know there's nobody I'd rather have. But with Alviso running loose, this is the more important way. At that, I don't expect we'll run across Sawtelle. I'm not fool enough to go after him with only two men to back my play. All I want is to find the place those horses were taken through the canyon."

In half an hour Dex and Shorty and Dolf were ready to ride. Wasatch was throwing a diamond hitch over the pack bulked on the back of the Oregon mare. Down the road from San Geronimo, Milly Duquesne came riding. She waved to Dex, who swung his horse and rode out swiftly to meet her, stopping her a hundred yards from the ranchhouse. He glanced at the well stuffed saddle bags behind Milly's saddle with satisfaction.

"This is great, Milly," he said. "You're going to stay for a while?"

"You bet," said Milly. "Dad has gone to Flag and will be gone a week. Sonia wanted me to stay last time I was out. I'm taking her up this time. Dex—what happened to your face?"

Dex shrugged. He knew it would do no good to try and evade the question. Milly was entirely too sharp of eye, too quick of wit to be fooled. "I'll let—her—tell you about that."

Milly's blue eyes sparkled angrily. "She—used a quirt on you?"

Dex nodded. "Maybe I had it coming."

"I think," snapped Milly—"that I'll change my mind about this visit. I think I'll go home."

"You'll do nothing of the sort. You'll go right on up to the house and keep your pretty little mouth shut—about these." Dex ran a finger over the welts on his face.

Milly's eyes softened. "You're just too darned generous to be real, Dex Sublette. But I'll go up to the house—and I'll not promise another thing. That young lady needs a dressing down—and I'm qualified to give it to her."

"Listen to reason," begged Dex. "I'll bet she's suffered a lot more than I did. Give her a chance. She's got a lot of things to forget. And I've seen you lose your head and get mad enough to use a club on me, let alone a quirt."

"I know your pride, Dex Sublette," said Milly quietly. "I know how you've suffered. Yet, because you've asked me, I won't say a word—unless she starts it. Then—she better look out."

"That's fair enough," conceded Dex. "Hear from Tommy, yet?"

"Look in my eyes, Dex—and see if you can tell."

Dex looked and smiled slowly. "You've heard. He's coming home."

"Right," breathed Milly. "He's coming home."

There was a tender, fierce glory about her as she said this. A queer wistfulness came into Dex's manner. The wonder of it—to possess the love of such a girl as Milly Duquesne.

"I believe," he said slowly—"that Tommy Quillian is the luckiest man who ever lived, Carrots. No man could ever possess a more precious thing than your love, Milly."

Quick tears started in her eyes and her mobile lips trembled. She reined close to him and put her hand on his. "The—the funny part is, old dear—I love you, too—but not—that way. Can you understand it?"

"Yes," said Dex. "I can, because it goes double, Milly. Funny how those things stand, isn't it? And now, because Tommy is on his way home—and because it won't be long before you'll be Mrs. Tommy Quillian—I'm going to say good-bye to the little, long-legged imp, who I've played with, fought with—and always loved. Do you think Tommy would mind if I kissed you, Milly?"

For a moment she stared at him, as though half frightened. But what she saw in his eyes quieted and relieved her. As she had always felt toward Dex, so he felt toward her. They were as brother and sister. She laughed and tipped up her face. Dex kissed her lips gravely. Then he reached out a long arm and rumpled her bare, red gold hair.

"Old brick-top," he chuckled.

Milly's laugh rang clear and happy, "Old square-toes, old deacon," she retorted. "Your good-bye is just—hello. Where do you think you're going with that pack-horse?"

"Shorty and Dolf and me are taking a look at Thunder River Canyon. We lost some horses down there somewhere. We're going to look for a trail. See you again in a few days. Be kind—to her," he added soberly.

"I will," promised Milly—"as much as I think is good for her. I think I understand. You're the kind who would wait all your life—for the one woman. And if this will make you feel any better, old dear—being a woman, I know how a woman feels. Only two reasons would ever make a woman use a quirt on a man. The first is if she hated him—and the second—is if she loved him. And I am very, very certain that Sonia Stephens does not hate you, Dex. Now see if you can figure that out. Hasta luego, compadre."

With another laugh and a wave, Milly rode on to the ranchhouse.

Standing in that ranchhouse, well back from a window, where there was no chance of her being seen from the outside, Sonia Stephens watched that meeting of Dex and Milly, and Milly's approach. Her face was wan and white, her eyes haunted with shadows. She had not moved when Milly and Dex first met and spoke. But when Dex had bent his head and kissed the laughing red head, a strange little half stifled gasp had broken from Sonia's lips. She had whirled then and walked back and forth across the room, beating her hands softly together in a gesture of unconscious perturbation and dismay. Yet, by some feminine legerdemain, when she opened the door to greet Milly, she had forced a smile of welcome to her lips and had veiled, in part at least, some of the haunting emotion in her eyes.

VII

Salty Simmons, station agent at San Geronimo, eyed the man before him with suspicion and disfavor. The morning overland had just pulled in and out of San Geronimo, leaving this man behind. Salty had little experience or interest in masculine fashions, but his lazy eyes widened, just the same, as he looked this new arrival over.

The fellow was in store clothes of a cut which Salty vaguely felt had some kind of a foreign flair, a dark suit. His shoes were pointed and of patent leather. His hat had a funny upward roll to the brim, with a colorful feather stuck in the band. And he carried a slender malacca cane.

That cane fascinated Salty. It was the first one he had ever seen. Salty covertly felt of his hip pocket, to make sure his purse was still there. This stranger looked like some kind of a tinhorn, in Salty's eyes—either a card sharp or a shell game artist.

The newcomer's age was hard to fix, except to the most discerning eye. Though slightly swarthy, his skin had the grayish, weathered look of a man fighting desperately but futilely against the remorseless march of the years. Massage and scrupulous care had kept that skin from wrinkling, but the years of the man showed about his eyes—black, cold, calculating eyes.

Those eyes went over Salty haughtily, almost with

contempt; at least, with open condescension. The newcomer inclined his head ever so slightly.

"Is it possible to secure a conveyance out to the ah—Pinon Ranch?" he asked.

"A what?" blurted Salty. "Out here we talk English, Mister."

"A vehicle—a wagon—"

"Oh," Salty grunted. "Why didn't you say so the first time? Yeah—I reckon you can hire a buckboard from Abe Connors, down at the livery barn."

"And this—ah—livery barn—where is it?"

"Straight down the street—at the far end. You can't miss it. Got a big water trough out front."

The stranger drew out a flat, gold cigarette case, extracted a cigarette and lit it. "You will have my luggage ready," he said, intangibly making of the words an order. Then he walked off, leaving behind a thread of smoke as foreign as his appearance.

Salty sniffed the odor of that smoke. "Ain't marihuana," decided Salty—"but it shore smells dopey to me. Some kind of a dang foreigner, I bet'cha. Maybe he's a Russian—some friend of that little princess lady out at the Pinon spread. But that little jigger of a cane—my Gawd—that cane. Lucky for him it ain't evening with some of the boys in town and a little warm with liquor. Else they'd have him out in the middle of the street right now, doing a jig in them shiny shoes of his. At that, those shoes wasn't so bad. Maybe I might get me a pair. Sort of tone a man up, they would. They shore were shiny."

There was a trunk and two suit-cases, which Salty piled at the end of the platform, whence soon Abe Connors took them, stacking them in the back of the buckboard. Then, with the stranger on the seat beside him, Abe set out for the Pinon Ranch.

At the ranch itself, Milly Duquesne was having rather tough sledding in trying to maneuver the conversation around to the subject of Dexter Sublette and those tell tale welts she had seen on Dex's face. Sonia was stubbornly reticent about such a subject and kept swinging the conversation into other channels. Finally, with a sigh, Milly admitted defeat and accepted Sonia's lead. They talked of lighter things and, though Milly's breeziness and good spirits won an answering gaiety from Sonia, always, deep in Sonia's eyes, there lay a queer shadow of grief.

Milly sensed a strange complexity of feeling in Sonia. She felt that Sonia was honestly glad to see her, but there were times when she sensed a bitterness in Sonia's manner also—and a wistful envy. It was all very puzzling.

The hours slipped by until just at midday, as they were about to sit down to eat, Marcia came bursting in, white of face. "Your highness—" she choked. "Serge—Serge Varoff—is outside."

Sonia went dead still. Every vestige of color drained from her face. "Serge—Varoff!" she breathed.

Marcia nodded frantically.

Sonia stood up, gripping the table to steady herself. She drew that full, elfin lower lip between her teeth, biting it cruelly. Then—"Serge Varoff!" she whispered again.

Abruptly she stiffened, her head lifted to a regal tilt and her face became hard and cold. "You will show him in, Marcia," she said quietly. Then, as Marcia went out, Sonia looked at Milly. "I wonder, my dear—if you would excuse me for a time? This—this is unexpected—and distressing."

"Of course," said Milly quickly. "I'll go down and eat with the riders. I've done it before. Are you sure— well, if this Serge Varoff is offensive to you—one of the men can quickly cure that. They'll send him packing in a jiffy."

Sonia shook her black head. "That would do no good—now."

Milly headed out. On the porch Serge Varoff stood. Abe Connors was just turning the buckboard for the drive back to town. Milly felt the impact of Varoff's cynical, rather offensive glance, but the fiery red head gave him one in return which brought a faint show of color into that grey, aged skin. A moment later Milly was out of sight around the house.

At Marcia's stilted greeting, Varoff smiled slightly, bowed and went into the house, his attitude reflecting a bored curiosity. When he stepped in to face Sonia his smile thinned and widened and grew mocking. He clicked his polished heels together and bowed very low from the waist.

"Your highness," he murmured suavely. "This is indeed a pleasure."

Sonia stood very straight, one hand spread against the base of her slim throat, the other gripping the edge of the table, as though for balance.

"Why have you done this?" she asked, her voice unsteady.

He raised his precise eye-brows slightly. "You would question my fidelity? My dear Sonia—you should know me better than that. Where the heart is—" He shrugged significantly.

"Yes," agreed Sonia coldly—"I should have expected it. It is your peasant blood, Serge Varoff—which gives you this blood-hound instinct."

His face darkened under the rush of blood and the mocking light in his eyes turned to a cruel hotness. "Insults will not help you, my dear Sonia. I think that it would be wise should we sit down and come to a thorough understanding."

"There is no understanding that I wish with you," flared Sonia. "In pursuing me as you have, you have violated every code, every tenet of a gentleman of honor. Have you no shame?"

"You forget," purred Varoff—"you forget that you are my affianced bride."

"That is not true," cried Sonia. "You are presuming on the edict of a regime broken and dead."

Varoff's eyes narrowed. "The wish of the Emperor—"

"You forget, Serge Varoff—that this is America. I—am an American. I am my own mistress—here."

"And you would forget—so easily."

There was just a trace of wildness in Sonia's laugh.

"Forget? Yes—willingly, willingly—For I see now with clear eyes. I can see the slavery—the monstrous cruelty of the edict of which you speak. Then—I was just another foil in the scheme of a tyranny that would use me to its own end. I was to be wed to a man old enough to be my father. My wishes were not consulted and, had not the revolution come as it did, I suppose I should have bowed my head before that edict and submitted. For such was the custom. But all that is gone, Serge Varoff. Here I am free—do you understand that—I am free. And there is no one who may tell me what I must do—except myself. You have gained nothing by following me here. In a way, I am glad you have come—for now I see the shadow which has followed me so long—I see it right before me. And in the clean light of this new world I can realize that that which I feared, I can laugh at. The threat which dogged my dreams is nothing more than a pitiable old man— drugged by dreams of the past when the name—Count Serge Varoff meant something."

It was a terrific indictment. No man could have been proof against it. Varoff fairly writhed and a red, sadistic rage built up in his eyes. Somehow he managed to control himself, though the effort left his face pallid with perspiration. He bowed again. "We will forget that period of the past." He was once more suave. "Perhaps I have been blind, as you say. And you have interested me with your enthusiasm for this new order of things. I would enjoy being your guest under these new surroundings."

Sonia hesitated, then nodded. "Very well. With that understanding—you may stay."

Far down on the flank of the great sage slope, Dex Sublette led the way in front of Shorty and Dolf. They were far enough into the haze and mists now to glimpse the great, yawning throat of the Thunder River Canyon. And it seemed that there was a persistent, distant echo—a dull, far off rumble which was present one moment, then gone the next, only to return as the air currents changed once more. This was the voice of the river, growing stronger as they neared the rim of the canyon itself.

"That danged canyon gives me the jeepers," Shorty confided to Dolf. "It's such a hell of a long way to the bottom. Wonder how a feller would feel if he fell in? Wonder what he'd be thinking about while he was tumbling about half a mile or more, with not a gol darned thing to hang on to except air?"

"You," growled Dolf irritably—"can think of the darndest things. With your imagination you should have been a fortune teller."

"There ain't no law against a man thinking, I reckon," grunted Shorty.

Here the sage slope began to run out into comparative level and the sage and juniper thinned almost to nothing, for the earth turned more to rocky shelves.

Dex reined in. "We'll split up here," he said. "You boys take the packhorse and head north. You can leave the packhorse at Concho Creek and we'll make camp there. Then I want you to work the edge of the canyon, careful. Look for sign. Sawtelle, or whoever run off with our broncs, didn't grow wings and fly across this canyon. There's a trail somewhere, a break in the rim that a bronc can go up and down. I'll ride south and look the country over down there. I'll meet you at camp around sundown. Use your heads and don't ride out on the rim of the canyon like Chuck did. You'll be asking for lead poisoning if you do. If you want to go right out on the rim, go on foot and pick a spot where you can have some cover. If you find a trail down, don't take it yet. We'll try it together—later."

All afternoon Dex rode, paralleling the canyon. He brought to bear all the cunning at reading sign which he had stored up in a lifetime. But nowhere could he find the break in the rim he was looking for. He covered at least ten miles before turning back. Once or twice he left his horse ground-reined a little distance back from the rim, and went out to the edge of the terrific chasm on foot, carrying his Winchester under his arm. Each time he selected a spot where he could use cover of some sort.

The canyon, Dex judged, was a good mile across. The upper rims were of sandstone, stark with color, uneven and broken with pillar and pinnacle, shelf and sheer wall. But as it dropped away, deeper and deeper, those shelves ran in toward each other and the canyon narrowed to a winding gash of shadow, deep into the granite heart of the earth, where the brilliant maroons, and browns—purples and yellows of the upper rims, dulled to a leaden grey that grew almost black in far, far depths.

Dex could not make out the tumbling wild waters down there, but he could hear the voice of it. It came up to him with a sort of ululating cadence, now faint, now loud—but always sonorous, always menacing.

Out beyond the canyon the Thunderhead Mountains climbed and Dex lingered, enthralled, as the sun crept from sight beyond the mountains, the colors of the canyon walls faded and the whole great chasm became a sea of deepening, violet mists. Soon it was impossible to see very far into the depths, for the shadows choked thicker and thicker and much of the canyon was gone, washed out by that violet tide. Only the sound of the water remained the same, hoarse and sustained—the real voice of the canyon.

Shorty and Dolf had picked a camp spot a good two hundred yards back along Concho Creek from the place where it met up with the canyon, to foam and slither and glide and finally leap into space. As Dex rode up he could smell the tang of wood smoke and soon picked up the red eye of the camp fire.

Shorty came out to meet him. "We found it, by gollies," he announced triumphantly. "And we found where that jasper was hid out that creased Chuck, last time we were here. We been looking in the wrong direction. We should have had sense enough to know that the slug never came from across the canyon. Shucks! No man could make any kind of a shot from that distance. The jasper who shot Chuck was holed up on this side the canyon, right at the head of the chimney the trail goes down. Dolf found the empty shell. We shore were dumb on that other trip."

Dex grinned wearily. "Dumbness, old son—is catching. You boys got the disease from me."

"Oh, I don't know," objected Shorty loyally. "We were all guilty of over-running the trail. We were too anxious to get a look into the canyon, I guess. And then, after Chuck got creased, we didn't have time to do much else but think of getting out of here with a whole skin. But we got a line on those suckers now."

After eating they sat for some time around the fire, smoking. There was little conversation. Though the camp spot was secluded and ringed all about with friendly willow and aspen, the presence of the canyon was almost over-powering. It was distinct, terrific.

You couldn't, Dex mused, find any unit of measurement which would fit a thing like this canyon. It was, after all, but a physical thing on the face of Nature, a structure of cliff and pinnacle, rim and ledge—and space. But it had a presence—which reached out and touched things. A mystic, stirring thing, that presence, which could shock the eye and daze the mind and bludgeon the imagination. And when anywhere near that presence, it took hold of you—subdued and humbled you—and made the talk of men, and the thoughts and trials, sorrows and joys of men, puny and inconsequential. For the lives of men were but clock ticks against the eternity of the canyon.

Shorty stirred restlessly and pinched out a cigarette

butt. "I got the jeepers again," he burst out. "That danged canyon. Can you fellers feel it like I do? I'm going to tie myself in the blankets tonight. Else I'm liable to get up in my sleep and take a run and a jump into that God-awful hole in the ground."

"It's your liver," growled Dolf. "Your system is loaded up with too much grease. Shut up and forget it."

"Wouldn't I like to," blurted Shorty. "But that canyon—it keeps whanging away at my mind. I tell you, I'm spooky as a bronc full of loco weed. I'm going to turn in. Maybe, if I get real close to the ground and sort of get a good hold on it, I'll feel better."

Shorty and Dolf turned in together in one of the soogan rolls, Dex took the other. Shorty's fears were groundless. He and Dolf were soon snoring. Sleep was reluctant with Dex. He lay for a long time in his blankets, his eyes wide, his thoughts winging. And the presence of the canyon faded to be replaced by the picture of a slim, black-haired figure, laughing in the sunlight.

The dying coals of the fire snapped open to bare a crimson heart for a time, before turning grey and dead under the moist touch of the night air. Through the cloistered greenery overhead the stars glinted, white and lonely. One of the horses stamped wearily—

"This is the place, right enough," declared Dex Sublette. "I'm going down for a ways. You boys wait here."

He took his Winchester and turned away on foot.

That canyon had Shorty whipped, but there was nothing wrong with his loyalty. "Only need one man here to watch the broncs," he said between set lips. "Dolf can do that. I'm coming with you, Dex."

They went down the steeply slanting rock chimney cautiously. Underfoot the rock was cut and scarred with the marks of shod hoofs which had gone up and down many times. The morning sun was still too low in the sky to do much with the shroud of gloom which lay in the canyon. It was a swimming sea of mists, purple and cold—mist which lay still in some places like some strange sea and in others, whipped and driven by winds spawned in the depths, the mist curled and drifted and boiled like smoke.

The chimney twisted sharply to the right and led out on a ledge, hidden from the rim above, and which went downward at a long, generous slant.

Shorty drew a deep breath. "This ain't so bad," he muttered. "Easy going here. But keep back against the wall, Dex. We're in shadow, but there's no sense in tempting some eagle-eyed hombre who might be up early."

Dex chuckled. "You don't trust anything about this canyon, do you, Shorty?"

"No sir, by gollies. I figure I got a reasonable share of sand in my craw—but things around here give me the creeps. I admit it. But to a man who knows it, this canyon is some hideout."

The ledge worked out on to a broad shelf, dotted here and there with hardy juniper. Here was earth again instead of rock. Dex looked up. Already the rim was far above, cutting sharp and clear against the morning sky. Here on this shelf the trail lay plain, cut to dustiness with the hoofs of horses. The trail led directly angling out to the point of the shelf.

Again came a sharp drop-off, a steep pitch down which made Shorty swallow convulsively and drag his spurs to make sure of each step. The trail wound a spiral way across the shoulder of the shelf. It was narrow here and on the outside the sheer drop was terrific. Dex looked at Shorty.

Shorty's face was pale and dripping with cold sweat. His eyes were staring and his lips but a thin line above the angle of his indomitably set jaw.

"Go back, Shorty," said Dex. "No sense in you punishing yourself like this."

Shorty shook his head. "I go where you go," he croaked.

They reached a cut back, where the trail worked to the right once more. Leaning against a rock which seemed to bulwark that cut back, Dex looked down. He jerked around at Shorty, his eyes shining. "Come here. This is your reward, old top."

Shorty moved out beside him, got a two handed grip on that rock and looked over. South, a rippling veil of silver drew a line down a dripping, slanting cliff. This was the waters of Concho Creek, gliding like molten silver to finally leap off in mist and spray to drop a thousand feet sheer, before piling up in a cauldron of foaming boulders. Here, the incredibly beaten water formed once more into the solidity of a stream, working its way past a green line of aspen and cotton-wood across a wide shelf and then disappeared in a final leap into the junction with the Thunder River, far down in the granite heart of the canyon.

But the real interest was not Concho Creek. There were rude cabins down there—a cluster of them, built of the straight white barked trunks of quaking asp and roofed with sod. They stood not far from that cauldron where the creek boiled after that first great leap. Near the cabins was a spread of pole corrals and in those enclosures, at least two score of horses. A thin ribbon of blue smoke curled up from the rock chimney of the largest cabin.

And then, as Dex and Shorty watched, men began to appear. Some of them went to the corrals. Others carried in wood.

It was too far for any sure identification until two more men appeared. Even at that downward angle it could be seen that one of those men towered above the other in height. And the shorter one wore clothes unmistakable even at that distance.

"Alviso," burst out Shorty. "That damned spig is one of those."

"Right," crisped Dex. "And though I've never seen Sawtelle, I've heard it said that he was a big man—much bigger than average. Shorty, we're learning things."

Presently all of the men went into that bigger cabin. Nearly an hour passed before they appeared again. Then some half dozen came out, went to the corrals and saddled horses. Again there was no mistaking the leader of this group. It was Don Diego Alviso. Once in the saddle, Alviso and his men rode north, straight up the canyon, where, still shrouded with shadow, Dex could make out a faint trail leading into the thinning mists.

"This," said Dex with satisfaction—"means many things. It explains a lot. You know how Alviso and his crowd have been known to drop out of sight for a week or ten days at a time. They've got another way into the canyon, farther north. They're tied in with Sawtelle and his outlaw bunch. And this is the main hangout. Where they might take rustled cattle is still a guess, but we'll find that out also—later—now that we have this lead. But I'll bet those stolen saddle broncs of ours are right down in those corrals. We're looking at our horses, Shorty."

"Which ain't going to do us any good, right now," Shorty grunted. "We can't go down and get 'em. We wouldn't have a chance."

"We're not going down—now. Sometime later, maybe, when we can pull a surprise. One thing is sure. We got the dead wood on Alviso. We've seen what we came to see. Let's go on back."

VIII

Dex and his two companions rode into the home ranch a little after midday. Up on the ranchhouse porch Dex could see three people sitting. He identified Sonia and Milly, but the third, a man, was a stranger to him. Milly waved and it seemed to Dex that Sonia's arm started up as though to follow Milly's lead. But the gesture did not finish. It was as though an impulse had touched her, only to be quickly stifled.

Wasatch and Chuck came over from the bunkhouse. "What luck?" asked Wasatch, who had a sober, muted look about him.

Dex told the story tersely. "A night sortie can surprise that hangout," he ended. "But we'd need more men than we got now. I'm going to ask permission from the boss to put on about four or five more men until we push Alviso and Sawtelle off the map. If it is okay with her, I'll send Shorty and Dolf to town to look for extra riders."

"Who's the gent up there with the women?" asked Shorty, ever the curious one.

"A gol darned duke or count or something," growled Wasatch. "He showed up yesterday afternoon. Abe Connors drove him out from town. He had a lot of luggage. Looks like he figured on quite a stay. Some old friend of the boss, I reckon."

"You don't need to look so gloomy over it," said Dex, darting a sharp glance at Wasatch's lugubrious countenance.

Wasatch shrugged. "His coming didn't seem to make the boss very happy. I took her and Milly for a ride last evening and that girl had something on her mind, what I mean."

"Yeah," nodded Chuck—"And while they were gone, this jasper came down to the bunkhouse and asked me more questions than you could shake a stick at."

"What kind of questions?" demanded Dex.

"Well, he wanted to know how much range our brand took in. He wanted to know how many stock we ran—and how many horses. He asked me if I had any idea how much the whole layout was worth. He shore was inquisitive—and all his questions had to do, one way or the other, with dinero—pesos—dollars."

"Maybe the boss is tired of this country already," advanced Shorty. "Maybe she's figuring on selling again."

Dex's lips tightened. The same thought had come to him. "None of us know—we're all guessing," he said briefly. "And after all it's none of our business. Take care of the broncs."

He went up the slope then, a tall, lean, dusty figure, the skirts of his chaps swishing, his spur rowels singing. He bared his tawny head as he climbed the steps. Milly had a bright smile for him and a jocular greeting. "What luck, cowboy?"

Dex smiled at her. "Good. And you?"

"Counting the days."

"Lucky old red-head. I don't blame you."

But when Dex turned to Sonia, the smile left his face and his expression turned somber and grave. "Sorry to bother you, ma'am—but I have something to report and some suggestions to make that I want your okay on."

It came to Dex that this was the first time he had faced Sonia since the time when she had swung the quirt. Her eyes played across his features with a certain haunted wistfulness. Her graveness was on a par with his. She nodded slowly. "Of course. First, I would like you to meet—Count Serge Varoff. I knew Count Varoff—in Russia. Count—this is Dexter Sublette, my foreman."

Dex started to step forward, his hand outstretched. But Varoff made no move to leave his chair and his only response was a casual nod. He might have been greeting a menial. Dark blood rushed across Dex's face and his mouth tightened. He dropped his hand and met the nod with one of his own. Then he ignored Varoff so completely that Varoff shifted in his chair rather irritably.

For some reason he could hardly understand, Dex made a quiet request of Sonia. "Could we step aside a moment? This matter of business—"

"Of course." Sonia was on her feet with a swiftness which brought a flicker of wise amusement into Milly's eyes and as Dex and Sonia left the porch and sauntered around into the shade of the cottonwoods, Milly looked at Varoff innocently.

"They would make a grand pair, wouldn't they, Count?" she remarked. "How handsome they look together."

Varoff straightened in his chair. "You are indulging in fancy, Miss Duquesne," he said.

"Think so?" drawled Milly. "I'm not so sure. And

Dex is just the sort that Sonia needs. He has the strength and understanding."

"Ridiculous!" snorted Varoff. "You forget that she is of royal blood—while this man Sublette is nothing but a—"

"High class American," broke in Milly crisply. "Which is the true hall mark of real men these days."

Varoff sneered, ever so slightly. "You impugn Sonia's good sense. She would never make such a ghastly mistake."

A flash of anger shone in Milly's eyes. She stood up. "Frankly—you've no idea how Dexter Sublette gains by comparison with you. He—is a gentleman."

And with this scorching broadside Milly hopped off the porch and swung away down the slope to talk to Wasatch and the other boys at the corrals.

Varoff glared after her, biting his lips with rage. He swung his head to see what had become of Sonia and Dex, but they had already disappeared around the corner of the house. Varoff sank back in his chair, his face a mixture of baffled emotions.

Back in the cottonwoods, Dex halted and looked down at his companion gravely. "The day before you arrived here," he said, "we lost about twenty of our best saddle stock. The animals were taken down into the Thunder River Canyon country. The other boys and myself trailed 'em that far, but lost the sign down in the sandstone ledges. While we were trying to pick it up again, somebody took a shot at Chuck—creasing him across the head. At the time it would have been foolish on our part to have tried to push the issue. So we drew off and brought Chuck home."

"Then that story which Chuck told of having been thrown from his horse and hurting his head on a rock was not the truth?" said Sonia.

"Chuck told you that so you wouldn't worry. You had just arrived here then, you know."

"I see. Go on."

"On this trip that Shorty and Dolf and I took, we found the trail the outlaws used, getting into the canyon. Shorty and I went down it far enough to locate the hangout of the rustlers. We saw horses down there—probably most of our horses. We saw—Don Diego Alviso down there—and Sawtelle, who is known to be an outlaw. The point is this. As it stands, this outfit isn't strong enough to go down and raid that hangout and get our horses back. We need more riders—and I want your permission to pick up four or five good extra men, to keep on the payroll until we've cleaned up Sawtelle—and Alviso."

Sonia considered gravely. "This—cleaning up—as you call it—means fighting—shooting—probably killing or being killed?"

"I wouldn't lie to you," said Dex. "It will mean—all of that."

"Then, you will not hire those extra men—you will not try to recover those stolen horses. We will forget all about them. We will leave—Alviso and this Sawtelle alone. I want no one injured—or—or killed, fighting for my interests."

Dex shook his head. "That is generous on your part, ma'am—but it won't do. We've got to go after those renegades—or they will come after us. If we let them get away with one raid, they'll come back and strike again. I don't crave battle any more than anyone else—but I know this country and I know the people in it. A man has to be willing to fight—or he doesn't last. I recommend you let me hire those extra hands."

"If any rider in my employ was hurt—or—or killed, fighting for my interests—I would never forgive myself." She was very, very sober.

"You miss the view-point of the boys, ma'am. They consider the interests of the Pinon Ranch—their interests. It is a matter of pride with them. If anyone hurts the Pinon Ranch, the riders feel that it is a personal thing with them. Any chance they may take, they regard as a matter of course. The boys—and I—will be very disappointed if you do not give us that permission."

She stared away with troubled eyes. Dex studied her covertly. Much of the sparkle and vivacity she had possessed when first she came to the ranch, was gone, now. Her eyes were strangely moody. Her face was slightly pale and her eyes full of troubled shadows. And her lips held a tired, almost wistful droop.

"You," said Dex gently—"are not finding much in the way of happiness, these days."

She started slightly and the faintest color tinged her cheeks. She did not look at him. "If I am not," she said steadily—"it is because of my own folly—in several things. And, thinking of that folly, I have decided that I shall let you do as you see fit—concerning the outlaws. You have shown—you know what is best."

Dex built a cigarette. He did it more to occupy his hands than anything else—to keep them under control. For again that old emotion had swept over him. Even in her wanness, her tired wistfulness, she was bewitching.

"Then," he said, a little unsteadily—"I'll go ahead and hire those riders. For I know, to exist—that we are going to have to fight. I'll go down and send Shorty and Dolf to town right away—after those extra men."

He started to turn away.

"Wait," she commanded.

She was twisting her hands nervously. But there was courage in her eyes as she looked up at him. "The marks of that—that quirt—are beginning to fade," she said. "And I am thankful—thankful. For the thought of them has haunted me and I have hated myself—so thoroughly. I was a contemptible little beast. And I am wondering, Dexter Sublette, if you could find it in your heart—to forgive me?"

She was utterly honest. And suddenly the galling harshness which had ridden Dex ever since he had felt the bite of that whip, was gone. He laughed softly. "If I owe you forgiveness, you have it—freely. That whole thing was a mistake, on the part of both of us. It is forgotten. Think no more of it—ma'am."

A lot of the misery went out of her eyes. That elfin lower lip trembled into the beginnings of an eager smile. "You—used to call me—boss. I—I liked that."

"Very well—boss." And he laughed softly.

"You are, very, very generous, Dexter Sublette. I think I shall be happy again, now."

They moved back into sight of the porch. Here Dex halted again. "If there is anything you would like me to do, in the way of entertaining your guest, the Count—don't be afraid to ask," he drawled.

Sonia looked at him closely. It was as though she had read a double meaning in those words. "Thank you," she said. "Knowing Count Varoff as I do, I am sure he will not hesitate to ask for his own entertainment."

Dex went on down to the corrals and Sonia returned to the porch. Varoff looked at her intently. And what he saw did not in any way increase his peace of mind. He had been thinking of what Milly Duquesne had said and now he saw a change in Sonia which was more disquieting. Since his arrival at the Pinon Ranch she had been subdued, wan—her eyes haunted and somber. Now there was color in her face again, the set of her lips had softened to a musing half smile and her eyes held a warm, inner glow.

Varoff lit one of his Russian cigarettes. "I trust, my dear Sonia—that you are not entertaining any thoughts of folly," he murmured.

"Folly? I do not understand." Sonia looked at him coolly.

Varoff gave a thin, smiling shrug. "Romance, unless judicially approached and selected, brings nothing but sorrow."

122

Sonia colored hotly. "Any romance which I might consider, is strictly my affair, Serge Varoff."

"I wonder," mocked Varoff. "It makes a rather impossible picture to me, my dear Sonia. Consider—Princess Sonia Stephanovich—and—a common American cowhand. Yes—it is humorous—very much so—and impossible."

Sonia knew a sudden, taunting recklessness. "I have found Dexter Sublette's arms very strong and very gentle," she flared. "And his lips hold the sweetness of truth—and honor. Also, the name Stephanovich I have forgotten. I am Sonia Stephens—American. You may make what you wish of that, Serge Varoff."

Varoff lunged to his feet, his face twisted in jealous fury. "You—you speak like a—a—"

"A woman who knows her own heart," cut in Sonia—"and who, God willing, will find courage to follow it. I could hunger for the love of a real man, Serge Varoff—instead of the smirking, cynical, mercenary attentions of such as you. There—you asked for the truth—and you have it. And now—you will excuse me."

She went into the house then, leaving Varoff in a white, shaking rage.

Two horses swung slowly over the rim of the little basin and came down the San Geronimo road toward the Pinon ranch buildings. A humped, uncertain rider bestrode the lead horse and a rope ran from this rider's saddle horn back to the second horse. Across the saddle of that second horse hung the limp body of a stricken cowboy.

Down the road they came, through the pale glamour of a late, lop-sided moon. They pulled up in front of the bunkhouse. That first rider swung slowly from his saddle, wavered drunkenly, then stumbled into the bunkhouse. It was Dolf. His face was drawn and white under a garish mask of dried blood. His hat was gone and his hair a matted tangle of blood and dust. Dex Sublette, playing three handed pedro with Wasatch and Chuck, came to his feet with a leap and caught Dolf in his arms.

"My God—boy—what happened?"

"Alviso," croaked Dolf. "Bushwhacked me—and Shorty. Shorty—outside—tied on his bronc. Get—get him. He's hurt—bad."

And then Dolf fainted, sagging heavily in Dex's arms.

Blistering broken curses, Wasatch and Chuck darted out. Dex carried Dolf to his bunk and laid him there. Wasatch and Chuck came in, carrying Shorty between them. Dex looked at them, his face tight and bleak. "Dead?" he rasped.

"No," said Wasatch. "But hit deep and plenty hard."

Dex cut away Shorty's vest and shirt. A blue hole, oozing blood, showed just below and slightly to the right of the base of Shorty's throat. Dex lifted him gently, thrust an exploring hand across the back of Shorty's shoulder. There was the warm clamminess of blood and a hole there also.

"A gamble," said Dex hoarsely. "But the slug went plumb through. Chuck—sand it to the big house. Get Milly—thank God for Milly—she's good at this sort of thing. Tell Hop we'll want hot water—scads of it. Wasatch, you saddle up a couple of fresh broncs. You and Chuck are ramming to town for Doc Arnold. Step to it. Time means everything."

Wasatch and Chuck left at a run. Dex, working in a cold, dread daze, had Shorty undressed and in the blankets when Milly and Sonia and Marcia burst into the bunkhouse. Sonia was pallid but steady. Marcia was whimpering and wringing her hands. Milly was grave and cool.

"Have they a chance, Dex?" she asked.

"Dolf is creased on the head—and all in. He'll be all right. You'll have to judge for yourself about Shorty. Here, I'll hold the light."

At sight of the blood Marcia crumpled in a heap, moaning. Sonia gasped, but kept her self control. Milly, very gently made her examination. "Unless he is bleeding internally, he has a chance," she said. "Tell Hop to hurry—hurry."

Sonia caught Marcia by the shoulder and shook her. "Be still, little fool," she said fiercely. "There is work to be done. These are—our boys. Go and help Hop."

Marcia stumbled out. Sonia seemed to steel herself. She went over to Dolf, loosened the kerchief from his throat and set to sopping some of the slowly welling blood from the angry gash along the side of his head. Her lips moved in soundless pity.

Hop came scuttling in, clucking worriedly. He carried a big pot of steaming water. Marcia, white but obviously determined, followed with more water and a bundle of white cloth and various bottles and jars of disinfectant.

They worked silently, Dex and Milly over Shorty, Sonia and Marcia over Dolf. Hop scampered back to the house for more needs, among them a bottle of whiskey. In his hurry he bumped into Count Serge Varoff, who was about to step into the bunkhouse. Varoff exclaimed angrily, but Hop paid him no attention.

Varoff moved up beside Sonia, saw that her slim hands were crimson and dripping, then spoke peremptorily. "This is no work for you, Sonia. Look at your hands. I demand that you leave it to others."

Sonia did not seem to hear. She paid him absolutely no attention. She spoke tensely to Marcia. "Hold his head higher, that I may get this bandage more secure."

"Sonia," began Varoff, his voice rising—"I say—"

Dex whirled on him, curt and savage. "Get out!"

Varoff straightened haughtily. "You'd dare speak that way—to me?"

Dex stepped toward him. "Get out, before I throw you out. You're in the way."

Varoff quailed before the stark, grim savagery in Dex's face and eyes. He backed to the door and stumbled out. Sonia flashed a glance at Dex, who was again bent over Shorty. There was a queer, warm joy in her eyes.

Soon there was nothing more to be done. The stricken men were bandaged, their wounds cleansed and sterilized as far as possible with the materials at hand. Hop came back with the whiskey. Dex edged a stout jolt of it between Dolf's lips, but Milly, supervising, would only allow a teaspoon full for Shorty.

"He must be kept still, very still," she murmured. "We do not want him conscious—yet. All we can do now—is wait."

Dex pulled a chair up for her and Milly sat at Shorty's side, watching him intently—feeling of his pulse, gauging the slow, labored rise and fall of his chest.

Dex looked down at Sonia. "I'm proud of you, boss," he said.

"That bandage," she replied—"It is not what it might be. But it is the first—the very first I ever made. These poor boys—" Her eyes swam with tears and she bit her trembling lip.

"They're stout lads—both," comforted Dex. "Saddle men are hard to kill. Keep your chin up. They'll make the grade."

He gave Dolf another jolt of whiskey. Dolf stirred and moaned, then his eyes opened, blank at first but soon strong with reason. "Shorty," he whispered—"old Shorty—?"

"Doing as well as can be expected, Dolf," said Dex. "We've sent for the doctor and Milly is caring for him until then. And you know Milly—she's as good as most doctors, herself. How's your head?"

Dolf grinned wanly. "Full of bumble-bees and sky-rockets. How about a long drink of water?"

Sonia gave him the drink. Dolf looked up at her. "Th—thanks, boss."

"Where did it happen, Dolf?" asked Dex grimly.

"Back at Sunken Wash. We rounded up four men in town—they'll be out tomorrow. It was just about dark when we hit Sunken Wash. Shorty was riding in front. About four shots were cut loose at once. They got Shorty first clatter, but missed me somehow. When Shorty fell, I went out of the saddle after him. I heard Alviso yell—I could tell that dirty coyote's voice in a million—and he brought his crowd charging in out of the Wash. I reckon they figured they'd got us both, seeing as how I went out of the leather right after Shorty did. But they found out different. I caught 'em against the skyline and lathered 'em with both guns. I know I got at least two of 'em—I saw 'em fall.

"They lost their salt then and cut and run for it, throwing one last shot. It did this to me." He touched his head. "They didn't come back, because that slug knocked me out and when I came out of it, everything was quiet. It was kind of tough, but I managed to locate our broncs, mine and Shorty's. I was scared Shorty was done for, and all I could think of was to get him home as fast as I could. So I got him into the saddle and tied him there. Then I came on in. That's all."

"And it was plenty, old settler," said Dex. "There's iron in your blood. Now close your eyes and take it easy. Doc Arnold will be here bye and bye."

Milly stayed by Shorty, Marcia by Dolf. Dex walked slowly out into the night, building a cigarette. Sonia followed him. Dex stood looking off in the direction of town, his face cold and bitter. Sonia spoke impulsively.

"I have been so wrong—so wrong in many things, Dexter Sublette. That fiend—that Alviso—And to think that I—I quirted—" Her voice sank to a whisper. Her throat was too thick for further words.

"That belongs to the past," Dex told her quietly. "And Alviso—he'll pay—plenty, for this night's work. I—I'm sorry I spoke as I did to your guest."

"And I am glad," cried Sonia fiercely. "Oh—he is contemptible, Count Serge Varoff is. He has followed me against my wishes—offended me— He is a mercenary, calculating beast."

Dex was amazed at what he was listening to. "If you don't want him around—you have only to say the word. I'll send him packing in a jiffy."

"I wish you would—I want you to. I want you to drive him out of my life forever. Listen to me, Dexter Sublette, so that you may understand. At one time I was affianced to Serge Varoff—not by my own consent—but at the edict of—an Emperor. Such things were done in Russia in those days. Marriage was not the sublimation of love—of trust and respect and affection—not in royal circles. It was ordered, to the end of strengthening the royal power. It was the product of politics and pompous internal diplomacy. Serge Varoff is old enough to be my father—yet they would have done this thing to me—they would have driven me against my will into the arms of a man I despise—whom I've always despised.

"Then came the revolution. I lost much in that revolution—I lost my father, and my country. But I gained the freedom of my heart. I fled Russia and I thought I was done for all time with Serge Varoff. But he trailed me. He followed me all over Europe. He was like some relentless blood-hound after a frightened rabbit. It was then I remembered America. I remembered the great, wide, free country I had traveled through when I was a little girl. It reached out to me as a haven of security.

"I had saved some family jewels out of the wreck. I sold them for enough money to buy this ranch. I thought that here, I was done with Serge Varoff. But no—even here he has found me. And it isn't me that he wants. The man is almost penniless. He wants what little wealth I might possess. I—I have told you much, Dexter Sublette. I—I don't know really why. You—you understand?"

"I understand," said Dex, very softly. "Varoff will leave—immediately—and never come back. You go in with Milly and Marcia."

She caught at his hands as he turned toward the ranchhouse. "Why—why are you so kind, so loyal to me?" she asked him, her voice throbbing with a deep, stirring music.

Dex's face was unreadable in the gloom. His tone harshened slightly. "I told you once—but you did not choose to believe."

He drew away and left her and stalked up and into

the ranchhouse, where lights were glowing yellow against the night.

Varoff was pacing back and forth the length of the living room, that room which had been so big and barren in the old days, but which had now taken on a color, a hominess, with its intangible atmosphere of delicate femininity.

When Dex stepped in, Varoff faced him, a sneer bristling across his face. "If you've come to apologize, I'll have none of it," rasped Varoff. "I accept apologies only from my equals."

Dex laughed harshly. "There will be no apologies offered. You're leaving this ranch—now—and for good. I'll give you ten minutes to prepare. Your luggage will be taken into San Geronimo—later."

Varoff's look became one of incredulity. Then he laughed. "This is a poor attempt at a joke, my man. Be off with you—do you hear? Be off with you."

In two steps Dex had him by the collar, whirled him around and flung him into a chair with a jar which threatened to snap Varoff's neck. "I'm not joking," he snapped curtly.

For a moment Varoff was stunned. Then he cursed, leaped to his feet again and darted a hand toward an inner pocket. It came away carrying the small, compact blue bulk of a foreign made automatic pistol. Before he could swing the weapon into line, Dex had him by the wrist and twisted the weapon free with a snap that left Varoff writhing with pain. Then Dex slammed him back into the chair again. "You're leaving this ranch,"

Dex growled. "Make your mind up to it."

Varoff became baffled, full of shrill hate. "The princess—Sonia—will hear of this—"

"I'm doing this at her request," cut in Dex coldly. "You'll save yourself a lot of grief by going out of here like a gentleman. Either that or be thrown out bodily."

Varoff realized the inevitable was at hand. There was no gainsaying the all too evident authority of this big, sun-blackened rider with the icy voice and eyes.

"But what have I done that I should deserve such treatment?" argued Varoff, trying to temporize.

"You know—you know all too well. But in America—at least in this part, hombre—we don't stand for any man annoying a woman. You've followed Sonia for the last time—you've annoyed her for the last time. Now you're leaving."

"You would throw me out—you would make me walk—to that ghastly town—that San Geronimo?"

Varoff's true age stood out all over him now. He seemed to shrivel, like a spider drawing in about its venom.

"I'll put you on a horse," said Dex. "I'll show you the road. If you follow it you can't miss San Geronimo."

"But after that—after that? Where will I go?"

"To the devil, for all of me. I'm through talking. If you've got some riding togs in your luggage, jump into them. You've wasted half that ten minutes already."

Varoff went to his room. He soon returned, in foreign cut riding breeches and boots. His face was pallid, his cheeks loose and hanging. He looked every inch the thorough rotter he was.

Dex led the way down to the corrals, caught and saddled a horse. "You can leave the bronc at the livery barn with Abe Connors. I'll pick it up later."

Varoff glanced over at the bunkhouse, where the lights were turned low and where tense waiting was in the air. "Could I have a word with Sonia—with the princess?" he whined.

"None," bit out Dex. He could see where Sonia might find pity for this whelp and then he would have the unpleasant job to do all over again. "She wants no further talk with you. You're going—and never coming back. That's all. Git!"

Varoff crawled clumsily into the saddle and started out. Dex waited until he saw the dark silhouette of horse and rider disappear over the rim of the little basin. Then he rubbed the palms of both hands vigorously against his chaps and strode to the bunkhouse.

IX

Serge Varoff rode slowly through the far night along the road to San Geronimo. For some time he was humped and still in the saddle, stunned and bewildered at this astounding thing which had happened to him. At first it seemed that all his faculties were numbed. He— Count Serge Varoff, literally thrown out by order of Sonia.

Of course, that big, crude savage could have been lying. Perhaps Sonia had said nothing of the sort. Perhaps that fellow Sublette had designs on Sonia himself. Varoff clung desperately to this thought for a while, for it salved his vanity somewhat to believe himself an object of another man's jealousy.

But as Varoff cast back, he knew that he was wrong. He remembered that when he had spoken to Sonia in the bunkhouse, when her hands were red with the blood of a wounded rider and her eyes were drenched with misty pity and grief, she had not even appeared to hear him. And when Sublette had ordered him from the bunkhouse, Sonia did not countermand the order.

Varoff roused from his apathy and a gust of shuddering rage shook him. He cursed and the oaths ran away with him. He applied them to Sublette—to that red-headed friend of Sonia's, and finally to Sonia herself. He raged and ranted and shook his fists at the still, wondering stars.

Out of the night ahead came the rush and pound of speeding hoofs. Fright caught at Varoff and he reined off the road and into the sage and junipers, where the fragrance of them caught at the throat with rich, aromatic tang.

Three riders roared past, their horses breathing in gusty, panting cadence, saddle gear creaking, heavy dust lifting in spurts under the pounding hoofs. Soon they were gone, leaving behind the reek of sweating horse flesh to vie with the scent of the sage and junipers.

Wasatch—Chuck—and Doc Arnold—racing through the night on their errand of mercy. . . .

Varoff pulled back to the road and went on. He

became conscious of the night, of the far, lonely darkness, of the slithering, pallid sheen of the moon. A slow fear of this great land consumed him. He cursed no more, but cringed lower and lower in the saddle as he rode. And when a coyote sent the echoes dancing from a nearby arroyo, Varoff cowered and shuddered.

"Alto! Halt!"

The words broke suddenly, in guttural vehemence.

Varoff hardly understood the words, but he understood the tone. He jerked his staid old cow pony to a stop. Of a sudden he was aware of the dark bulk of massed riders before him in the middle of the road.

"Quien es? Who is it?" came the demand.

Varoff, thoroughly terrified, gulped and licked his lips. "I—I do not understand—" he faltered.

There was a burst of gruff cursing and then mounted men were all about him. The reins were jerked from his hands—talon fingers bit into his shrinking shoulder.

"What is this we have found. Pedro—a light!"

A match snapped into flame and was thrust almost into Varoff's eyes. He cringed, crying out in terror. Dimly from the glow of that match he saw peering faces—swarthy, brutal faces.

The light went out. "Caramba!" growled a voice. "It is in the form of a man, yet it cringes and cries out like a trapped rabbit. This is poor game we have found this fine night, amigos."

"Would it have water or good red blood in its veins?" said another. "Stand aside, Juan. My knife is keen this night. I would try it on that shrinking throat."

"And the good Don Diego would have your ears for it. Back! Poor as the prize is, we will take it with us. It is for our patron to decide what shall be done with it. See—it is near fainting. Pah! That such a thing should ride as a man. Tie it to the saddle, quickly!"

Varoff's hands were seized and his wrists bound tightly to his saddle horn. And then, palsied with fright, he was carried on through the night, for long, bone-wrenching miles, the passage of which he was too drugged with fear to notice. There was grisly mockery in the wail of the coyotes who complained of the passage of those hard spurring riders.

"Give it to us straight, Doc. What are his chances?"

Doc Arnold looked up at Dex Sublette and shrugged. "It is one of those things, Dex. My opinion, either way, isn't worth a plugged cent, right now. If I had to say something, I'd say his chances were even. One thing we do know. By some miracle, none of the heavy arteries were cut. If they had been, he'd have been dead long ago. Shorty has lost a lot of blood, but he's a tough, hardy little devil. There's always a chance for a fellow like him. Time will tell the story. We've done everything possible."

Doc Arnold, a tall, spare man of middle age, with greying hair and kindly, shrewd eyes, turned back to his patient again, caught Milly's eye and smiled.

"You run along and get some sleep, Milly. I'll make a night of it here and in the morning you can take over."

Milly nodded and stood up. Dex turned to Sonia and Marcia. "That is a good suggestion for all of you ladies. Run along and turn in. We can give Doc all the help he needs. You've been fine, all of you. Collectively, we're mighty proud of you."

Milly and Marcia went out. Sonia lingered a moment at the door. "Serge Varoff?" she murmured.

"Is gone," said Dex. "I don't think you need ever worry again about Serge Varoff."

She hesitated, looking out into the darkness. Then she gave him a grave smile. "Thank you, Dexter Sublette," she said simply.

Dex went back and sat down beside Doc Arnold. Wasatch and Chuck were prowling restlessly about. Dolf was quiet—sleeping under a mild opiate the doctor had given him. "You fellows turn in," Dex told Wasatch and Chuck. "You give a fellow the jeepers, as Shorty would say. Doc and I will hold the fort."

It was a long, long night. The light was turned low and soon the silence of the outer dark came in to claim the bunkhouse. Wasatch and Chuck, after tossing for a while, drifted off. And Dex Sublette and Doc Arnold watched the dreary hours through. From time to time Doc Arnold would lay careful fingers on Shorty's pulse and watched the signs of mounting fever with a critical eye. The still, dead hours of midnight came and passed. With their coming Doc Arnold grew grave and watchful, but as they went by and the cool, wet odors of the dawn crept in the open windows, the frown left his brow and he slumped back in his chair in relief.

"He's climbed the toughest part of the trail," he murmured to Dex. "Once they lick those death hours, as I call them, they're generally good for another day. And when a man shot as Shorty is, gets by one day, he's liable to make the grade. Optimism is legitimate right now, Dex."

Dex went out and had a smoke, while the misty grey dawn broke over the world. He was weary and gaunt, but some of the lines which had formed in his face smoothed out. Dex knew real affection for the happy-go-lucky, garrulous Shorty. He glanced up at the main house, still and slumbering. "She's meeting the test," he murmured. "She was a little Spartan when Dolf first brought Shorty in."

In the east the sky began to light up, to turn silver and rose. Things which were but shadows a moment before became distinct and solid. A slow wind stirred, bringing with it the scent of sage and juniper and the creosote-like tang of tar-weed, dew drenched and redolent. Somewhere down the creek a cow bawled plaintively. A thread of pale smoke crept up from the kitchen chimney of the ranchhouse. Faithful little Hop Lee was up and about his business of getting breakfast. Dex went up there to beg a cup of hot coffee.

"Little Talk-talk?" asked Hop briefly but anxiously, which was Hop's name for Shorty.

"Coming along in good style," Dex told him. "Doc is feeling pretty confident."

"Velly good," chirruped Hop, pouring the steaming coffee.

There was a stir at the inner doorway and Milly Duquesne stood there, an old dressing gown wrapped about her, her coppery hair tousled, her eyes lazy with sleep.

"I smelled the coffee," she smiled. "How's chances, Hop?"

"Can do," chuckled Hop, setting out another cup.

"You look tired, and yet rested, Compadre," she said to Dex. "So I know that Shorty is coming along. Right?"

"Right. Doc's feeling a lot better about him."

"Doc," said Milly, "is regular."

"I can name others," drawled Dex. "You, for instance—and Sonia and Marcia. With such nurses, I expect Wasatch and Chuck to go out and try and stop a slug."

"You should try it," dimpled Milly. "I'm quite certain Sonia would take over that job all herself. She was rather splendid, wasn't she?"

Dex nodded. "She'll make a hand, yet."

"What did you do with Varoff?" Milly asked abruptly. "You didn't take him out and kill him, did you?"

Dex chuckled. "I put him on a horse and started him for town—with orders not to come back. I don't know why, but I enjoyed that chore. Sonia—Miss Stephens gave me permission, you know."

"I'm glad," shrugged Milly candidly. "He was a louse."

"Your language," said Dex sternly, "is a whole lot less than elegant."

"I don't care. Nobody could feel elegant about a man like him." She set down her cup and headed for the inner door. "Tell Doc Arnold I'll be down to relieve him in a few minutes."

Wasatch and Chuck were up, busy at the morning chores. Dex went down to help them. "What are you going to do about Alviso?" demanded Wasatch.

Dex's jaw clicked. "Wipe him out at the first chance."

"Me," said Chuck—"I ask nothing better than the chance to string that spig on a slug. He's caused us too much trouble as it is. And he'll kill somebody yet, if we don't put a stopper on him."

"This range ain't near big enough to hold him and us now," said Dex grimly. "That was raw, shooting down Shorty and Dolf like that, without no cause or reason."

"When a snake like Alviso goes on the bite, he don't wait for cause or reason," growled Wasatch. "Say— that's funny."

"What is?" demanded Chuck.

"I'll swear I saw that little old claybank cutting bronc that Bill Ladley used to ride, in the cavvy corral with those other broncs, last night—just before dark. And it ain't there now."

Dex smiled thinly. "I guess that must have been the bronc I put that Varoff hombre on last night when I gave him the run."

"Varoff! You mean that count or duke jasper?" Wasatch demanded.

"Yeah. I sent him on his way last night after you boys had gone for the doctor."

"The devil! And what will the boss have to say about that?"

"She told me to."

"I'm a son-of-a-gun!" Wasatch chuckled. "Good for her—good for her. He had a bad eye, that hombre."

Serge Varoff was very near collapse. He was bruised and battered and wracked from long, unaccustomed miles in the saddle. Mentally he was in a foggy daze, his mind numb from the bludgeonings of fear. He had no idea of the direction his captors had ridden, nor how far. And when they finally did draw up before some shadowy ranch buildings, Varoff was almost too far gone to notice that they had stopped.

His wrists were freed and he was jerked roughly from the saddle. His legs buckled under him and he fell to the ground. Boots drove into his ribs and he was lashed with curses. Clawing hands hauled him to his tottering feet and he was half shoved, half dragged into a building, where his staring eyes blinked dazedly at the yellow light of a guttering candle.

Sounded the interplay of guttural voices. He was pushed into a chair and a cup of searing liquor held to his lips; Varoff strangled and gulped but some of his strength came back. His head lifted.

Facing him was a lithe dapper individual in velvet bolero jacket and bell bottomed trousers. A dark face and cold, black eyes surveyed him and the thin lips beneath the waxed black mustache writhed into a bleak smile.

"You feel better, senor—no?"

Varoff bleated weakly. "Villainous treatment," he panted. "Savage brutes. And I have done nothing—nothing—"

"You have been staying at the Pinon Ranch?"

That liquor was running all through Varoff's veins now, warming and strengthening him. And it gave him a false courage. His mind cleared.

"Yes. I have been a guest at the Pinon Ranch. This outrage—"

Don Diego Alviso held up a mocking hand. "My men—they are rough at times—but their hearts are big. They are not bad fellows when you know them." His laugh was more of a hiss.

Varoff shuddered. "They were brutes. They bound me—they beat me—"

Again that indolent hand stopped him. "Tell me, senor—what brought you on such a lonely ride through the night? Where were you going when my good men found you?"

Varoff cursed. "I was going to San Geronimo. I had been ordered from the ranch by that devil, Sublette—and with the consent of the princess—"

"Ah!" Don Diego leaned forward, his eyes glinting. "They did not treat you well, then?"

Varoff was feeling much better. Apparently he was not to be killed after all. Here was a man who wished to be friendly—an understanding fellow who would appreciate the indignity of his predicament. The bottle of fiery liquor was on the table. Varoff took it and gulped greedily at it. And in Don Diego's eyes, as he watched, was the feline glint of a tiger about to pounce. But Varoff did not see that.

"Would you," he cried—"call it being treated well, to be driven from beneath a roof by a common devil like Sublette? I—Count Serge Varoff—to be threatened and abused by such as he?"

"But you say the princess—it was with her consent?" murmured Alviso.

Varoff cursed. "That little fool. I am not done with her—yet. I—"

"Tell me," broke in Alviso—"are there riders missing from the Pinon Ranch? Two riders, for instance?"

"Two riders?" Varoff blinked. The raw aguardiente was getting in its work now. His brain was beginning to fuzz up. "Two riders. There were two who came in—both wounded. I hope the fools die. I hope—"

It was Don Diego who cursed now. "Dios! Those gringos are hard to kill. They cling to life like a miser to his gold. With my own eyes I saw one of them fall, with the limpness of death about him and with my own hand I fired the shot. And now you tell me he was not dead. Perhaps, senor—you are lying to me."

His black eyes bored at Varoff, dancing with cruel, vicious lights. As for Varoff, he was partially drunk. He bristled.

"Always I am being insulted by you common cattle," he shouted, pounding the table with his fist until the candle wavered and danced. "First it was Sublette—

then those crass brutes who brought me here. And now by such as you. I am Count Serge Varoff—do you understand that? I demand the respect due me. I demand—"

Varoff broke off suddenly. Even his alcohol inflamed senses were not impervious to what he saw. It was the round, blue muzzle of one of Don Diego's big guns, staring at him across the table top. And even as Varoff watched, pale flame bloomed from that menacing steel eye and the room shook to the thunder of report. Count Serge Varoff flung back in his chair, wavered a moment then slipped limply to the floor, shot through the heart.

Don Diego Alviso stood up coolly, walked around the table and flung open a door. "Juan! Pedro!" he called crisply. "Come and drag this carrion out of here. And you will have the men saddle fresh horses. There is work to do."

X

Doc Arnold finished strapping on his voluminous saddle bags, then stepped into the saddle of his fleet, steel-dust mare. Dex Sublette stood at the doctor's stirrup, his hand outstretched. "I'm thanking you for the whole outfit, Doc," he said.

The genial doctor smiled. "Rather thank the ingrained toughness of that little monkey, Shorty," he said. "It is a never ending source of amazement to me—the punishment you saddle men can take and come up smiling. I'll stake my professional reputation right now on Shorty's getting well. He is coming along amazingly. So I leave him in the hands of the most charming set of nurses it has ever been my privilege to observe."

Sonia was there and Milly and they laughed their thanks. They waved as Doc Arnold rode off.

At that moment a rider came over the rim of the basin and dropped down along the road. Behind him he led a riderless horse. Dex frowned.

"That looks like Billy Oakes, who works for Abe Connors," said Milly.

Billy Oakes was a freckled, tow-headed youngster of sixteen and he grinned bashfully as he came up. "Here's a bronc that belongs out here, Mr. Sublette," he said.

The horse was the staid little claybank pony that had been a favorite of Bill Ladley. It was the horse Dex had started Serge Varoff out on the night before, for town.

"Varoff leave it at the stable, Billy?" asked Dex, as he took the claybank's rein.

Billy shook his tow head. "Dell Hanson run across this bronc out about four miles from town early this morning. He was on his way to town, Dell was—so he brought it along and left it at the stable. Abe, he told me to bring it home."

"Four miles from town," murmured Dex. "That's queer. I wonder was the bronc heading home when Dell found it?"

"I don't think so, Mr. Sublette. You know the trail

Dell generally travels from his ranch to town. It was out somewhere in those tar-weed flats. Dell said the bronc was out there kinda working around in circles, like it wasn't quite sure just where it was."

"I see," said Dex. He flipped the boy a dollar. "That for your trouble, Billy."

The boy grinned, ducked his tow head and reined about. "Thanks, Mr. Sublette." Then he lifted his own horse to a jog as he started back for town.

Wasatch and Chuck came out of the bunkhouse. "Well," grinned Wasatch—"anyhow, that Varoff gent didn't turn horse-thief. I see he sent the bronc back."

Dex frowned. "The strange part of it is, Wasatch—he didn't send it back. This bronc was found, early this morning, out in those tar-weed flats along the trail to Dell Hanson's spread. Dell ran across it himself and took it along to town. Billy Oakes just brought the horse home."

Wasatch scowled. "You figure that Varoff feller run into trouble out there somewhere—that he got lost, or something?"

"I don't know what else to think."

Dex looked at Sonia, caught the look in her eyes, and nodded. "We'll go out and look for him," he said quietly. "He might have got lost or he might have been thrown—or got off to rest and forgot to ground-rein the horse. Either way, we'll go out and find him and see that he gets to town safe."

Sonia drew a deep breath. "Thank you. After all, we wouldn't want any harm to come to him."

"That's right," said Dex gravely. "We wouldn't. Saddle up, Wasatch. You and me and Chuck will go out and find him."

Wasatch and Chuck went off, grumbling. "Damn tender-foot," muttered Wasatch. "We'll probably have to ride to hell and gone to find him."

"I hope he broke his neck," said Chuck. "Me—I never did like that jasper."

Dex went into the bunkhouse with Milly and Sonia. Dolf, his head swathed in bandage, was sitting up. Shorty was still unconscious, but his breathing was better and his color not too feverish. Milly took his pulse and nodded. "Very good," she murmured. Then to Sonia—"No need of you staying here, my dear. You go and get all the rest you can—for tonight will be another long one, and we'll have to stand shifts. I'll get some rest this afternoon."

Sonia nodded and went out, casting a swift look at Dex as she passed. But Dex was talking to Dolf in low tones and did not notice.

"You say you got the Edwards boys, Joe and Slim— and Ben Rellis and Jumbo Dell—to agree to ride with us, Dolf?"

"That's right," said Dolf. "Ben and Jumbo will be out tomorrow, but it will be near the end of the week before Joe and Slim can show. They had to go way up north of the railroad and help old man Crellin bring in a shipment of beef stuff to the cars. Soon as that job is done, they'll be out here. I'm just as well satisfied. For that means by the time they show up, I'll be ready to fork a saddle and throw a gun again. And I shore want to be in at the showdown against Alviso and Sawtelle. Me—I got an axe to grind." And Dolf looked over at Shorty.

Wasatch stuck his head in the door. "Broncs are ready," he announced.

Dex went out and the three of them rode away along the town road. As they topped the basin rim, Wasatch ran his keen old eyes over the far reaching miles of the range. "If that hombre had a ounce of brains, he'd set up a smoke signal of some sort. But he'll be too damn dumb for that. He'll bat around crazy like and end up by flopping somewhere and we'll probably ride right by him. Believe me, I know. I've hunted for lost pilgrims before. We got a job on our hands."

They rode as far as Sunken Wash, where a hovering circle of buzzards led them to two dead horses. Saddles and other riding gear had been stripped from the dead animals and they lay there stiff and grotesque, already badly swollen from the heat.

"Too bad Dolf had to waste his lead on broncs," said Wasatch. "I reckon this is the spot where him and Shorty ran into those damned greasers."

Dex nodded. "Dolf showed a lot of the old salt, taking that smash across the head and yet managing to bring Shorty in. And he was shore he got a couple of Alviso's crowd, but Alviso must have lugged the bodies off with him. Anyhow, Dolf and Shorty were lucky—plenty. So far we've had a lot of good breaks. Our luck can't hold that way forever."

As though in answer to this, Chuck pointed north and east to where a low, sugar-loaf ridge shoved a tawny head up through the surrounding mat of sage and juniper. "More buzzards," he said succinctly.

Sure enough, winging their slow, gruesome circle about the sugar-loaf ridge, were several ominous black dots. "Maybe another horse that got crippled and run that far before it went down. But we better make sure," said Dex. "Come on."

They drove their horses through the sage and juniper then up the sharp slant of the sugar-loaf. Dex was the first to reach the top and as his horse reared and snorted, Dex froze in the saddle, staring at the shelf of rock which crowned the little peak. Wasatch and Chuck pushed up beside him.

"Gawd!" blurted Chuck. "It's him!"

Spread-eagled across that surface of rock lay the body of Count Serge Varoff, his dead face to the sky. Across the front of his shirt spread an irregular reddish black blotch. There was no question that he was dead.

Dex dismounted, wordlessly. He stepped over and examined the body gravely. His first thought was that Varoff might have gotten thrown by his horse and then, being lost, had gone wild with fright and killed himself. But he saw immediately that this could not have happened. The road was down there—a good two miles of it in plain sight from the top of the sugar-loaf. To follow it either way would have meant finding people. And there was no weapon anywhere about, for Varoff to have used on himself, even had he wished to.

"Been other broncs up here," announced Wasatch, who had been riding a slow circle about the sugar-loaf. "Here's where three or four came up this side."

"The answer," said Dex, his voice flat and cold—"is plain. Varoff was killed, then carried up and left here. Whoever did it knew that buzzards circling this little peak would catch the eye of anybody riding along the road. They wanted this man to be found. And there's a certain mockery—a certain damned cruelty about it that tells just one name."

"Alviso!" growled Wasatch.

"Alviso," snapped Dex. "He's turned into a damned, murdering wolf."

"Look yonder!" cried Chuck.

They whirled, to see him pointing down toward the road. A single, madly riding figure was thundering along the road, a figure crouched low in the saddle, with a bright fan of copper gold hair whipping out behind.

"Milly!" exclaimed Dex, his voice queerly strangled. "It's Milly. Something's wrong at the ranch."

He was into his saddle with a leap and spurring his horse wildly down the slope. At his heels Wasatch and Chuck came slashing. Dex barely reached the road in time to head off the madly riding girl.

At sight of him she set her horse straight up. Her face was set and white, but tears were blinding her eyes. "Dex!" she sobbed. "Oh—thank God! Dex—they've got her—they've got her!"

"You mean—Sonia?" Dex's voice was little more than a croak.

"Yes," wailed Milly. "Alviso. Oh—Dex, Dex!"

Milly was near collapse. Dex put an arm around her and shook her. "Steady—steady, old girl. How did it happen?"

Milly clung to him. "Not—not over half an hour—after you left. They came down—from above the house. I was in the bunkhouse—watching over Shorty. Marcia had just come down, with some breakfast for Dolf. Sonia was alone—except for Hop—in the big house.

"I—I heard her scream. I ran to the door. Alviso and two of his men were dragging her from the house. They had come down quietly from in back. Hop—poor little Hop—he came out at them with a butcher knife, fighting for his mistress. And they shot him down, Dex. They killed Hop.

"Then others of Alviso's crowd came—they came toward the bunkhouse. But Dolf—I screamed to him—Dolf got out of the blankets, grabbed a Winchester and opened up. He killed three of Alviso's crowd. The rest broke and rode for it then, Dex. And they took—Sonia—with them."

The flesh on Dex Sublette's face seemed to shrink and harden—his eyes to draw back in his head. "Which way did they take her?" There was nothing to his voice but the words.

"Down the creek toward the Thunderheads. Dolf—Dolf wanted to go after them—alone. But I made him stay—somebody had to stay and defend Marcia—and Shorty. And I came to find you. Oh

Dex—we've got to do—something!"

"We will," Dex gritted. "You go on into town. Spread the word. Tell Abe Connors. Tell him to get every man who can ride and shoot and to head out to the ranch. I'll leave word there what they're to do. That's all. Fly!"

Obediently and without further waste of words, Milly streaked on for San Geronimo. Dex said nothing to Wasatch and Chuck. But he rode like a madman, driving his foaming bronco to the last ounce of its speed and strength.

To him, there seemed no life within him. He was like some burned out clinker, driven by a surface energy that was cold and relentless and mechanical. He took no notice of the brown earth flowing back beneath the blurred legs of his horse, he saw none of the familiar landmarks as they whisked past. His eyes were fixed straight ahead and he rode far up over the horn of his saddle, as though his own bleak energy would lift the bronco to higher speed.

The beating wind flattened the brim of his sombrero back against the crown and Dex's profile seemed compressed, almost hooked, so tight and drawn were his lips. His face looked bony and hard.

His horse was faltering in its stride as it finally tipped the rim of the basin and tore down the slope toward the ranch buildings. Without expression Dex's eyes flitted back and forth. Out there in front of the ranchhouse lay a flat little bundle of cloth—which was Hop Lee, the valiant little Chinaman, who had died in fruitless defence of his mistress. All in a close huddle lay three other dead men—all Mexicans—those of Alviso's band whom Dolf had cut down with his Winchester. And Dolf was now in the doorway of the bunkhouse, rifle cradled in his arm.

Dex left his saddle while his horse was in mid-air of its last frantic plunge. He struck running and reared to a tall, tight halt before Dolf.

"Milly," Dex snapped. "We met her. She told us. I sent her on to town to spread the word and round up more men. She'll bring them back to the ranch. When they get here, you got to be an iron man, Dolf. You've got to lead them down to the trail into Thunder River Canyon. Alviso has gone that way. Wasatch and Chuck and I are going on ahead."

"I'll show 'em that trail if it kills me, Dex," promised Dolf. "The damned wolves."

Wasatch and Chuck came pounding up. Dex whirled on them. "Saddle three fresh horses," he rasped. "Pick the fastest in the cavvy. Step on it."

Wasatch and Chuck raced for the cavvy corral. Dex stepped into the bunkhouse. Marcia was there, crouched beside Shorty's bunk. At sight of Dex she began to whimper. Her eyes were wide and dark with terror.

"Mr. Dex," she wailed—"Sonia—my mistress—"

"I know," said Dex gently. "We'll bring her back. You've got your work to do, here." He nodded at Shorty. "Be a good little trooper."

From a cupboard in one corner of the bunkhouse,

Dex broke out numerous boxes of ammunition, both for rifle and revolver. He apportioned these among three sets of saddle bags and carried the bags out to the doorstep. He got three canteens and filled them. And by that time, Wasatch and Chuck were there with the fresh horses. As a final thought, Dex included a pair of field glasses with his own duffle. As he gathered up the reins, he spoke once more to Dolf.

"If we're not at the head of the trail, you'll find us in the canyon—somewhere. We're riding this trail to a finish."

"I'll be there," promised Dolf.

Dex whirled away and spurred down the creek trail and out ahead of him he could see the blue bulk of the Thunderheads spiking the sky. They seemed, in their majestic calm and aloofness to mock at the puny griefs and trials of men. Dex glued his eyes to the trail and sank in the spurs.

The trail left by the renegades was easy to follow. Not once did Dex slow his pace, even when the sign crossed the limpid riffles of Concho Creek and led out toward the great sage slope. Alviso knew that men would strike his trail—men vengeful and grim—men who would ride that trail to the last show-down. And so Alviso wanted the sanctuary of the canyon before he would turn and fight.

The three riders went down that slope, where the grey sage ran out into the mists and heat haze—toward that last cold depth which was the Thunder River Canyon. Behind them the tawny dust funneled up and spread, a plaything of the vagrant wind. The sleek sheen of the horses turned dark and rough as the sweat started and ran and the foam began to gather and roll about the edges of the saddle blankets.

Not once did Dex speak, nor did Wasatch or Chuck. The same grimness was in their faces, the same hawk-like intentness in their eyes. Only, far back beneath Dex's scowling brows there was a queer, broken look, a torture of the soul—an inner suffering that left him haggard and savage.

Abruptly the sign Dex was following swung at a northern angle across the slope, cutting back toward Concho Creek. It crossed the creek and then split, some of the sign going straight north, the other tracks turning once more down toward the canyon.

Dex pulled in and pointed, as Wasatch and Chuck came up beside him. "They've split," he croaked harshly. "The damned clever devils. And God—I don't know which trail to follow."

There was something in his words which caused Wasatch to reach over and lay a hand on Dex's arm. "Steady, kid—steady. If you think, this doesn't fool you a bit. Alviso don't dare go anywhere else with that girl except into the canyon. Traveling north from here with her would be a strong gamble of running into white men who would ask how come and why for, even if they hadn't heard of the raid. And Miss Sonia would soon put them right—which would mean Alviso's scalp. And he knows it. We'll go on down to the canyon."

Dex knew that some decision had to be made, so he bent to Wasatch's canny reasoning. He followed the sign leading down. And soon, hardly more than two hundred yards beyond the spot where the sign had split, the judgment of Wasatch was vindicated. A tiny crumpled ball of white cloth lay there in the sage. Dex leaned far over and swept it up, without stopping his horse. He opened it, spread it in his hands. It was a filmy handkerchief—Sonia's hankerchief.

"You see," growled Wasatch triumphantly. "That game little girl is nobody's fool. She knew that Alviso was trying to mix up the trail and somehow she managed to drop this handkerchief to show which was the right way. Hats off to our princess. It takes real salt to keep your head and think like she's done, in the kind of jam she's in. Sand it up, Dex. We're going into Thunder River Canyon."

Now through the shifting mists, they could glimpse the great multi-colored maw of the canyon and they lifted their mounts to one last, tearing burst of speed. Dex knew where the head of that trail lay; it was marked by the jumble of sand-stone out-crops which had hidden it cunningly. He headed for that cluster of broken stone.

Wasatch pealed a shrill warning. Out of those rocks, dead ahead, a figure had reared upright—a dark and lowering figure in the dress of one of Alviso's renegades. The fellow had a rifle at his shoulder and, even as Dex glimpsed the weapon, he saw a spike of pale flame leap from the muzzle.

The head of Dex's horse tossed wildly and he felt the brute begin to go. Frantically Dex kicked his feet from the stirrups and flung himself aside. Then the stricken horse, shot through the head, crashed down—while Dex lit rolling amongst the stunted sage.

XI

When Sonia Stephens went up to the big house, after seeing Dex and Wasatch and Chuck start out in their search for Serge Varoff, she had known a certain qualm of conscience. Dismissal of Varoff from the ranch could have waited until daylight, when he would have been more certain of finding his way to San Geronimo. Now he was probably lost.

But Sonia's sense of pity did not endure very long. She thought of the weary miles she had traveled, trying to rid herself of the distasteful presence and attentions of Serge Varoff—at the callousness he displayed in scoffing at her wishes, at her pleading to leave her alone. And then she grew a little fierce.

This western country was beginning to influence her, to mould her—in a way to harden her. She thought of last night—last night when Dolf had come in with Shorty, hanging limp and seemingly lifeless over his saddle. She thought of the grim, stricken silence of the other men of the outfit as they looked at their wounded comrades. She remembered the way she had worked at Dolf's wounded head, how her hands had grown warm and slimy with blood. Yet she had not weakened, nor shirked her duty. Indeed, she had known a sort of fierce pride in the knowledge that she had found strength and courage to meet an emergency. Yes—this western country was already at work on her. And so, she soon lost all sense of worry over Serge Varoff's predicament.

She knew she could trust Dex Sublette to find Varoff. Dexter Sublette was that way. You could trust him in all things. Her eyes grew warm as she thought of him—warm and a little wistful. When she had poured out her story to him the evening before he had listened quietly and then gone to send Varoff on his way—to see that she was freed forever of Varoff's unwelcome attentions and persecution.

But these thoughts brought a pang with them. She had caught at Dexter Sublette's hands and had asked him why he was so good—so faithful in her trust. And his answer had twisted her heart. "I told you once—but you did not choose to believe."

Those were the words he had spoken and Sonia knew full well what he meant. That night—now clothed in such rich robes of romance—that night when strange and thrilling words had broken from Dexter Sublette's lips—words of a love that had waited through the years for such as she . . . And then his lips—on her own. And her quick anger and blighting words of contempt and reproach.

She could still sense how he had drawn within himself—how the warmth had left his eyes and voice—how he had grown hard and cold and distant. She had destroyed something that night—crushed out a warm flame which it seemed would never light again. Her lips quivered and she blinked at the sudden mist that blinded her. She went slowly to her room to rest.

Marcia accompanied her and fluttered about for a moment. Then she had left, saying that she was going to take some breakfast down to Dolf.

Sonia found that rest was a little bit difficult to achieve, despite the fact that she had slept very poorly the night before, and felt wan and listless at the moment. The savage, grim side of this western land had shown itself in wounds and blood and near death. And her nerves were still rough and edged because of it.

She lay with her eyes closed, vaguely conscious of the drowsy sounds about the ranchhouse. In the kitchen she could hear the clank of pan and pot and the high, chirruping tones of Hop Lee, faithful little Hop Lee as he talked to Marcia while preparing a breakfast for Dolf. Outside her window, on the nodding tip of a cottonwood an oriole was singing. . . .

She must have dozed a bit. At any rate, she did not hear the rush of heavy feet until they were right at her door. The next moment that door burst open. Sonia screamed. She couldn't help it—for the room seemed filled with swarthy, snarling renegades. Leading them was Don Diego Alviso.

There was no suave, smiling politeness about him now. Instead, his expression was more vicious and feral than the rest. He snarled orders in Spanish. Rude, brutal hands seized her, muffled her struggles, carried her through the house and out into the open, where other renegades waited with ready horses. She was flung into a saddle and tied there.

With horrified eyes she saw Hop Lee come running, waving a butcher knife he had caught up in his kitchen. Guns blared thunderously about her and she saw poor little Hop rear to a stop as though he had run into an invisible wall. His feet twisted grotesquely and his head fell limply sideways. Then he pitched forward on his face.

She saw renegades spurring down toward the bunkhouse, where two wounded men lay and where two kindly women were caring for those men. She caught a glimpse of Milly Duquesne's red gold head in the doorway. And then Milly was pushed aside and a lean cowboy stood there—a man with his head swathed in bandages. But he had a rifle at his shoulder and the snarling, thin crash of it began to whip across the horrified morning. Sonia heard lead strike soddenly—once, twice—three times. And in rapid succession she saw three renegades whirl and pitch from their saddles. The rest veered off and with her in their midst, roared past the bunkhouse, past the feed sheds and corrals to go thundering down the basin toward the west and south.

For a time Sonia seemed to lose all count of everything. It was as though she rode in a stupor, almost a faint. But the rack and drive of the horse beneath her, brought her sharply back to the realities of the moment. On one side of her rode Don Diego Alviso, on the other a blear eyed, fang toothed ruffian. There were other riders in front of her—in back of her.

Her jumbled senses began to clear, her stunned thoughts to function. She began to think. This raid had been perfectly timed. It had come when Dex Sublette and Wasatch and Chuck were absent on their search for Serge Varoff. It had been too perfectly timed, just to have happened that way. Somehow she knew that the warped brain of Alviso had planned it.

She looked back and knew another gust of horror as she remembered how Hop Lee had fallen and pity swelled in her heart for the faithful little Chinaman. And after that pity came a surge of blinding anger at these conscienceless brutes who had stolen her from her own home.

The virility of the West had worked more strongly on Sonia than she had guessed. Her immediate fear left her. Her head lifted proudly and her eyes, as they met a sidelong glance from Don Diego, were flaming with scorn and contempt.

"You filthy, rotten beast," she cried.

"Quiet!" snarled Alviso, lifting his quirt. "Quiet, or I use this on you."

They had been paralleling Concho Creek. Now they swung sharply to the left and splashed through the shallows and out into the sage on the other side. Sonia remembered this country. Out there ahead lay that great sage slope, the one Dex Sublette had taken her to view on that day when they had ridden together.

Her heart leaped at the thought of Dex Sublette. Orderly process of thought told her that it would not be very long before Dex Sublette would be storming along the trail in pursuit. For back at the ranch was Milly—Milly who knew this West with the practical view-point of a man. What had happened at the ranch would not leave Milly Duquesne in the throes of helpless terror. Already, no doubt, Milly would be riding for help—to find Dex Sublette and others. Yes, pursuit would soon be under way.

They were roaring down the sage slope now and, in spite of herself, Sonia knew a fresh chill of sudden terror. That great country ahead and below, so terrifically distant and wild—how easy it would be for Alviso and his renegades to find hiding there—and how difficult for their trail to be followed. But Sonia fought that gust of terror back and fixed her mind on the one thought that Dexter Sublette would not be misled. It seemed that she could almost see him, roaring along that back trail, his face a grim, indomitable mask. And there would be Wasatch, his kindly old eyes set and cold and merciless. And Chuck, silent, easy going Chuck, who would be a third avenging shadow—

Sonia had been riding, taut and tight strung with tension. She realized that every slim muscle was aching from that tension. So she relaxed in the saddle and found that this relaxation seemed to clear her mind and her eyes. She made a calm survey of these renegades riding about her. The scorn in her eyes deepened. She knew that these men were afraid, now—afraid of the wrath and the retribution which they knew would take up the trail. It was as though they envisioned the tall, sun-blackened figure of Dexter Sublette, coming down upon them like some ominous shadow. In the last analysis she knew that these men were cowards—all.

Ahead, though the drifting mists, she began to pick up flares of color and she sensed the presence of the canyon. Out beyond, still seeming as far away as when viewed from the ranchhouse, the Thunderheads lay blue and drowsy against the far sky. Sonia thought, irrelevantly enough, of what Dex Sublette had told her about distances in this western country—how the Thunderheads might look ten miles away but were really seventy. One had to live in this country to read the true values of distance—and of men. . . .

The renegades swung back once more toward the green marked course of Concho Creek. Here, where the pitch of land was so steep—the waters of the creek were foaming wildly as they slid, and leaped and crashed downward, as though with every foot their impatience for the meeting with the distant river increased.

The horses would have stopped to drink, but the riders spurred them ruthlessly across. On the far side there was a momentary halt. Don Diego snarled swift orders. The group split in half, one of those halves heading north, paralleling the canyon, the other half, with Sonia in the midst of them, turning once more down the slope toward the canyon.

Sonia understood what was being done. The trail was being split in the hope that the inevitable pursuit would be puzzled, thrown off stride, held up and delayed. Her mind cast frantically about. If there was only some way in which she could leave some mark—some sign, which would show the true trail. But her wrists were bound to her saddle horn. . . .

She looked down at those wrists, chafed and swollen by the cruel stricture of the rawhide thong which bound them. Her hands felt numb and clumsy—almost useless. Yet she could move her fingers slightly. And as she moved them she became conscious of something that had been clasped in her right hand—was still clasped there. It was a little, balled up piece of sheer linen, wrinkled, wadded and damp with perspiration. A handkerchief!

Of course—a handkerchief. She had had it clasped in her hand when she lay down to rest, back there at the ranch. And such was the unconscious force of habit, she had clung to it all through the whole period of fright and horror and wild riding. Furtively she opened the stiffened fingers of her right hand as far as possible. The motion of her horse did the rest. The handkerchief worked free and drifted down into the dust. Sonia sent a little prayer after it.

Now the canyon was right before them and the sensation of terrific space made Sonia queerly dizzy. Don Diego Alviso ordered another brief halt. Three of his remaining men swung from their saddles and with rifles in hand, scattered among a group of jagged sandstone boulders. Then Don Diego himself caught the rein of Sonia's mount and went on. Other men followed with the horses of the three renegades who had stopped among the rocks.

For a moment all seemed secure and stable under Sonia. Then her senses reeled and swam. Right before her the earth fell away into blinding depths. It seemed to her that the earth itself was twisting and writhing as it sheered precipitously downward. Muted sound boiled up, a somber, ululating ominous rumble. It was as though the canyon was speaking, in a thunderous, muted growl.

Sonia felt her horse tip downward. She slid forward in the saddle until the bucking rolls jammed hard against her thighs. For a moment she felt as if she were going to pitch headfirst over the saddle horn. She leaned far back, closing her eyes and some of that roaring in her ears she knew was the thundering of her own wildly beating heart. A ghastly sense of inner sickness swept over her. She had to bite her lips to keep from crying out.

Her horse lurched and slid and shod hoofs squealed against slippery rock. But the horse did not fall. In what seemed to the terrified girl a violation of all laws of gravity, the animal kept its feet and presently, with a snort of satisfaction, the animal leveled out.

Sonia drew a shuddering breath and opened her eyes. Here the earth was fairly level once more and the sense stunning space of the canyon was momentarily gone. For to the left the point of a shelf lifted and to the right that first terrible rim reared sheer and stark against the sky. But the trail wound on, angling across the shelf and then out over sheer depths once more, where sheer sandstone walls reared to her left, while to her right there was nothing at all—nothing but shimmering space and the rising growl of the canyon.

Sonia thought she must have fainted then. At any rate she remembered little of the rest of that terrible journey above those ghastly depths. She knew that there were times when even the horse seemed to stop breathing, but this came to her in a sort of subconscious sense—a thought hazy and half formed.

The end of it all came at last. Her horse stopped, seemed to relax with a gusty sneeze of relief. And there were the voices of men all about her, excited, coarse and profane.

She opened her dazed eyes once more. Here was a magic change. Here was earth—level earth, green with a sparse, tough grass. Here were trees, green foliaged trees—quaking asp and cottonwood. There were cabins, rude and rough, but stable enough. And here were men, almost a score of them, it seemed. They were all about her and she felt the impact of their eyes, hard and savage and evil.

There was one man who towered above the rest. He was gaunt and heavy of rib with a big, bony face with protruding lips and eyes and a tremendous, ugly beak of a nose. He had a hoarse, rolling voice and he shouted down the babble about him. He came swinging forward with a heavy, pigeon-toed gait until he faced Don Diego Alviso and was but a stride or two from Sonia's horse.

"What the devil is the idea, Alviso?" he rumbled. "What are you going to do with that woman?"

Alviso smirked and shrugged. "I have an eye for beauty, Senor Sawtelle. This lady—"

"You're a coffee-colored, ignorant fool," roared Sawtelle. "You ought to know better—but you greasers—you never learn. Hell, man—this means we'll have every available man within a hundred miles of here out after us. We had a tight little hangout here and were doing right proud by ourselves. Now you have to go and steal a woman. For a cent I'd rub you out."

Despite the roaring tones, Sonia could see that this man was not merely a blustering, loud mouthed bully. She could see that he meant what he said—that he was furious with anger and in those staring, repulsive, frog-like eyes there lay a half formed decision to draw and smoke Alviso down, then and there.

All of Alviso's smooth, oily suavity came to the surface. It was plain that Alviso was afraid of this man, that he wanted no battle or show-down with him.

"We have stolen many cattle—many horses, you and I, Senor," he said. "Why worry about the theft of one lone woman?"

"Because with women it's different," bellowed Sawtelle. "You can steal a man's horses or his cattle and he'll only fog a trail so far. But when you steal a woman, there's no trail long enough or far enough to take you plumb away. Men who hate each other's guts will take a trail together in a case like this. I might have known though, that something like this would happen. I was a fool ever to have tied in with you in the first place."

Under Sawtelle's railing anger and disgust a certain temper showed in Alviso's eyes. He spoke stiffly. "If such is your feeling, Senor—I will take my men and continue up the canyon trail."

"No you won't," snarled Sawtelle. "You've laid a trail right down to this camp and if you think you're going to sneak out and leave me to take the trouble alone when it arrives, you're loco. You're staying right here until I think this proposition out. And it's barely possible," he ended with a leer—"that I'll be interested in the lady myself. She's a likely looking filly."

Sonia could not hide her shudder of repulsion. These two, arguing over her, before that pack of savage eyed renegades. It made her physically sick.

Her wrists were freed and Alviso lifted her from the saddle. Wherever his hands touched her it was as though white hot irons had been applied to her shrinking flesh. She wavered on her feet slightly, but when Alviso would have supported her, she pulled haughtily away from him, her head high, her white face set and proud and defiant.

She was taken to one of the cabins. Alviso, with a mocking bow, opened the clumsy door for her. She went in and the door swung shut behind her. It was pleasantly cool and dusky in there and there was a rude bunk in one corner, unblanketed but piled deep with some kind of an aromatic wild grass, dried and rustling.

For a time Sonia kept her feet. Free for the time at least of those searing, leering eyes, her pose of defiance left her. Her shoulders drooped and she hid her face in her hands. It would have been a vast relief to have given way to grief, to the storm of unholy fears which tore and racked her. But she told herself that she must not weaken, that she must not break down and have these fiends discover her broken and weeping. She had to bear up—to keep her wits—to think and hope.

Some inner sense told her that she must keep her poise and courage, that she must fight for time. A lesser woman might go to pieces, to wail and beg and become hysterical—but not she, not she.

Somehow she knew that such a demonstration would arouse nothing but contempt in these renegades, while dignity and poise and cool courage might awaken in them some vagrant spark of respect and chivalry.

Don Diego Alviso she knew was utterly beyond the pale. He was cruel and treacherous and utterly vicious. But these others—even Sawtelle, might be handled and coerced some way. She had to keep her wits—she had to try.

She sank down upon the bunk and fought her thoughts into cooler, less troubled channels. For the time at least she was safe. Sawtelle, savagely angry with Alviso, had said that he must think the problem over—and while he was thinking out that problem, Alviso would hardly dare come near her.

Her thoughts lifted out past that high rim of the canyon, back along those hot dusty miles of the great sage slope, back to the Pinon Ranch, where little Hop lay dead—where a battered, wounded cowboy, his torn head swathed in bandages had winged death from an unerring rifle to exact payment for Hop's heroic sacrifice. And Dexter Sublette—where was he? Was he still out searching wide miles for Serge Varoff, all unconscious of what had happened—or was he pounding down the trail of pursuit and retribution for Alviso and the other renegades?

Steps sounded outside and the door swung open. Alviso was there—and Sawtelle. They came in. Sonia remained as she was, seated on the edge of the bunk. Her face was white but composed, her eyes level and unafraid.

Sawtelle rocked his huge self across the room and stood, his feet widely spread, his beaked face thrust forward, staring with bulging eyes down upon her. For a second Sonia's newly determined courage ebbed. What chance had she of awakening any spark of pity or chivalry in this repulsive looking monster? But she must try—she must try!

"Alviso," boomed Sawtelle harshly—"Alviso claims you're really a sort of friend of his—that you wanted to make up with him, but that Sublette wouldn't let you. How about it?"

"Alviso," Sonia answered, her tone low and composed "is a liar and a scoundrel. I despise him utterly. And I wish, on the day that Dexter Sublette beat him so terribly—that he had killed him."

Sawtelle guffawed hugely. He swung his heavy head around and mocked at Alviso. "The lady seems to know her mind and it shore sounds like she hates your coffee colored hide, my friend."

Dark blood congested Alviso's face. "I will see that she changes her tune, Senor."

Sawtelle laughed again and looked at Sonia once more. "You're in a tight spot, lady."

"I do not think so," answered Sonia boldly. "For you—you are a white man. You do not prey on helpless women. You have no quarrel with me—nor I with you. One may expect such things from his sort—" her glance at Alviso dripped with contempt—"but not from a white man, such as you."

Sawtelle's frog-like eyes blinked in clumsy thought. Sonia, watching him closely, knew that she had kindled a spark. "Yes, you are a white man," she impressed once more—"while Alviso is a—I think the word you used—a greaser."

Alviso, his face black with fury, took a step toward her. Sawtelle thrust out a huge arm and blocked his way. "No you don't," he bellowed. "Don't you touch her. Maybe there is something in what the lady says."

Now Sonia made the cleverest move of all. She jumped up and moved over beside Sawtelle. It was as

171

though she definitely sought his protection, that she was putting her trust in him, because he was a white man. She even laid a soft little hand on his great, gorilla-like arm. "We are white—you and I," she said simply.

The thought pleased Sawtelle—it pampered his ego, salved his conceit. It unconsciously pledged her his protection—from Alviso, at least. What Sawtelle's thoughts and actions toward her later on might be, she refused to consider. But at the present it was Alviso who must be subdued and outwitted. And her gamble won.

"Lady," promised Sawtelle ferociously. "If that greaser so much as lays a finger on you, I'll cut his heart out. Hear that, Alviso—you stay away from this cabin. This little lady hates the sight of you. Don't you come near her—if you aim to keep on living."

Bewildered dismay and savage anger fought for possession of Alviso's swarthy face. The anger won. His lips peeled back until his white teeth gleamed like the fangs of an animal. His eyes turned beady and red. He crouched slightly, as though he contemplated going for his guns. But cold reason told him that he had no chance in such a play. Even if he could beat Sawtelle to the draw and cut the unwieldy giant down, Sawtelle's followers greatly outnumbered his own crew and the life of himself and his men would inevitably be forfeit. This was no time for violence— open violence. The smart thing, the wise thing was to wait, to bide his time—to scheme this thing through, rather than try and battle it through.

He straightened slightly. The animal-like snarl on his face was replaced by a set, tight smile. He shrugged. "We will not quarrel, Senor—you and I. No woman is worth a rift in our friendship. I need your support—you need mine. No—we shall not quarrel."

He turned then and left the cabin. Sawtelle looked down at Sonia, his froggy eyes turning a little queer and unsavory. Sonia moved quickly away from him, waving at the bunk. "If this is to be my prison," she said—"surely I may have a few comforts. A blanket or two, perhaps—and water to drink and wash with. You will see that I get them, of course—for you are kind."

For a moment Sawtelle stared at her, his clumsy mind uncertain. Now that his initial anger at her presence in the camp had faded, he was becoming increasingly aware of her slim, exotic beauty. The animal was close to the surface in Jeff Sawtelle, but it had pleased him to have the girl step to his side in preference to Alviso. And it pleased him at this moment to carry out the character she had bestowed upon him. After all—the canyon was deep and his strength in it was great and time had a way of remaining constant.

"You bet," he bellowed hoarsely. "A lady is entitled to some comforts. I'll see that this cabin is made as snug as you please."

He swaggered to the door. Sonia went a little weak. She had won the first round—but what of those to come?

At that moment, carrying in through the open door,

came the thin, faraway snarl of a rifle. On the heels of it echoed a whole ragged burst of firing, while the echoes rumbled across the canyon and faded to nothingness in the vast distance.

In the doorway, Jeff Sawtelle stood motionless for a long second or two. Then he lurched out and his roaring voice bellowed across the camp, cursing and raging in warning.

As for Sonia, she stood with her clasped hands at her throat, her eyes wide and shining with a new hope. "Dexter!" she whispered. "Dexter Sublette!"

XII

That crashing fall into the sage as his horse was shot from under him, jolted and dazed Dex Sublette, and for a moment or two he lay there, twitching. On the heels of that surprise rifle shot came a snarl of fury from old Wasatch and then a rolling blur of reports as Wasatch threw two belt guns in savage cadence. Dex did not see that first renegade go down—but he did, as the lead from Wasatch's guns criss-crossed in him.

Dex got to his knees, stumbled to his feet. Both Wasatch and Chuck were shooting now and Dex saw dark figures running and dodging through those masking rocks. He snatched out his own gun and went to work. There were two of those figures and abruptly both of them were down and still.

The shooting stopped. Wasatch whirled his horse over toward Dex. "Hurt?" he cried anxiously.

Dex shook his head. "Jarred up a little. Those snakes were guarding the head of the trail. You and Chuck didn't get hit?"

"Nary hit. They didn't have time. We cut down on 'em too quick and straight. What next?"

"We go into the canyon."

Luckily, in falling, Dex's stricken horse had lunged out onto its right side, so that Dex's Winchester, slung under the near stirrup leather, had not been harmed. He dragged the weapon free and loaded his pockets with cartridges from the saddle bags, passing the remainder up to Wasatch.

"Okay," he snapped. "I'll lead the way. If those three whelps were the only guards left at the trail, we won't have any trouble for a ways. I'll go first."

"Bring our broncs?" asked Chuck.

"Yeah. We'll need 'em. Come on."

Dex went down that first sheer chimney swiftly, soon outdistancing Wasatch and Chuck, who had to take it more easily with the horses. Dex was savagely alert against surprise now. Luck had favored him up above. Had that shot which killed his horse been held a little higher, it would have certainly cut him out of the saddle like an empty sack. And there was more luck in the fact that he had been able to kick free of the stirrups and dive into the sage instead of being dragged down with the horse and perhaps rolled on. He was grimly intent not to blunder into another ambush.

But the way was clear, and when he moved out of the bottom of the chimney and across the casual slope of the first shelf there was no movement or sound anywhere, except for the deep, far voice of the canyon.

When Wasatch and Chuck emerged from the chimney on horses which scrambled to level earth once more with gusty snorts of relief, Dex saw that Chuck was a little pale around the gills, while Wasatch's jaw was set like a bear-trap.

"Tighten your belts," Dex said curtly. "It gets worse as you go down."

They swung around the shoulder of the shelf, skirted the sheer drop-off and came to the security of the first switchback. Dex slithered out on the rock bulwark and looked down. In a glance he knew that the alarm of that shooting up on the rim had reached the outlaw stronghold. Down there Lilliputian figures were running back and forth. Dex turned his head.

"Give me those field-glasses, Wasatch."

The powerful glasses, as he screwed them into focus, brought the scene up close to his eyes. He saw the huge figure of Sawtelle, the outlaw leader, rush from one of the cabins, waving his arms. Heavy and bellowing as was Sawtelle's voice, it could not carry that distance above the muted roar of the distant river. But Dex knew that Sawtelle was shouting orders.

Dex swung the glasses back and forth, grimly intent. It wasn't Sawtelle he wanted to see—it was Don Diego Alviso. For where Alviso was, there Sonia would be. For a moment the ghastly thought came that he and Wasatch and Chuck had taken the wrong trail after all. Perhaps that handkerchief had been, not a sign from

Sonia, but a clever ruse by Alviso, to make a lead on a false trail, while he had taken Sonia, not into the canyon proper, but north along the rim of it.

Then Dex's tight breath hissed out in satisfaction. He picked up Alviso. Alviso had darted from the crowd and was haranguing with Sawtelle. And Dex saw Sawtelle swing a giant fist and knock Alviso down and gallop past him with clumsy feet, while he organized his men for defence.

For Dex saw that Sawtelle was going to make a fight of it. He wasn't going to run, to try and find some other hideout up along that faint trail which crept north under the towering walls. For the time at least, Sawtelle was going to make a stand of it.

No horses were being saddled, but soon there were men, carrying glinting weapons in their hands, hurrying to various points about the camp. One group of a good half dozen came straight toward the wall of the canyon and disappeared under the over-hang. These men, Dex reasoned, had been sent to bottle up the trail, perhaps to advance up it and meet the threat then and there.

And now Dex caught a movement in the open door of one of the smaller cabins, off to one side. His glasses steadied and a strange, choking cry broke from his lips. It was a cry of relief, of triumph, of the bursting of long tension. A slim, dark-haired figure stood in that doorway. It was Sonia. Either by accident or design, she had shown herself and the sight of her was a message of trust and confidence to Dex. Yet, even as he watched, one of those scurrying renegades raced for that cabin, waving his arm threateningly. Sonia vanished from the doorway and the renegade slammed that door and seemed to lock it by some crude means. Then the fellow took up a place before the cabin, as though to guard it.

Dex turned to Wasatch and Chuck. "She—she's down there," he said, a little unsteadily. "And she's all right. I saw her for a moment, standing in the door of one of the cabins. But they've locked her in now and have a guard in front. Sawtelle and Alviso don't seem to be getting along very well. Sawtelle just knocked Alviso down with his fist."

"They must be kinda spooky," said Wasatch.

"They're excited, all right," nodded Dex. "But they're not running for it. They're going to make a fight of it. Sawtelle has sent a bunch out toward where the bottom of the trail must be. We're going to meet that crowd, somewhere between here and the bottom. There's no use in trying to get those broncs down, seeing as Sawtelle is going to make a stand of it. And they'd probably pick 'em off on us, long before we got to the bottom. So take 'em back up where the shelf opens and leave 'em there. Then we go on down, on foot."

While Wasatch and Chuck turned the horses and started back up with them, Dex renewed his work with the glasses. Things were more orderly down there now. As though recovering from the first fear of a surprise attack, the renegades, those which were still in sight, moved more leisurely. One of them, an old, hunched fellow with a long, white beard, showed with a bundle of blankets under one arm and a pail of water in the other. He clumped a bent-legged way across to the cabin where Dex had seen Sonia, talked with the guard, unlocked the door and went in. He soon came out, empty handed and went about his business. The guard relocked the door and took his post once more.

Dex knew the relief of a great let-down. The torture of uncertainty was gone. Sonia was down there and, though a horde of renegades and outlaws stood between her and liberty, he at least knew where she was and he was himself in a position to battle something more tangible than a dusty, hoof chopped trail through the grey sage for her deliverance. That dry, taut feeling of threat had left him, but the cold, grim determination to fight through to one final big clean-up did not waver.

One thing puzzled him. Why had Sawtelle clubbed Alviso to the ground the way he did? There were only two possible answers that Dex could reason out. Either the two outlaw leaders were at logger-heads over possession of Sonia—or Sawtelle disapproved of Alviso bringing her to the canyon camp and thus bringing also hard riding, grim jawed men to shoot it out in winning her back. If the forces of the law triumphed in the battle coming up, then Sawtelle would be through, in the Thunder River Canyon country, at least.

Wasatch and Chuck came back down the trail, their spur rowels ringing on the rock. "Anything new in the set up?" asked Wasatch.

"Nothing, except that they must feel pretty confident of holding the fort. I saw one of them take blankets and water to the cabin where Sonia is being held."

Wasatch looked like a grizzled old wolf, so bleak and set and savage was his expression. "Let's go," he said.

They started on down the trail, Dex in the lead. They did not hurry. Every step they took was onto new ground to them. This trail might be an old story to the outlaws, but it was new to Dex and his companions. Chuck was a trifle breathless.

"It's one God-awful ways down," he said, his voice jerky. "I'd hate to go over the edge."

"The steeper the wall, the less chance they have of getting gun sights on us," said Dex. "They can't see us from below. For that matter, they may not even know we're coming down. Maybe they figure the guards at the top of the trail stopped us."

"They know," growled Wasatch. "If we'd have been stopped up above, somebody would have been sent down to report about it. They're expecting us, all right."

In places the trail was hair-raisingly narrow, in others comfortably wide, but always it led down, down into the depths—from one switch back to another, drawing a rough and gigantic zig-zag pattern across the canyon wall.

High and higher the wall lofted above them and more than once Chuck tipped his head and squinted upward. "Me," he grunted. "I wasn't cut out for this billy-goat stuff. Give me level ground to ramble on. Should somebody who wasn't friends happen down from above, we'd kind of find ourselves in a jack-pot—sort of squeezed together between hell and what have you."

As if in answer to Chuck's thought, the thin, high crang of a rifle rippled its way along the painted crags and something which sounded like a vagrant wasp buzzed down, slashed along the inner wall not far from Dex and glanced out to crash itself to pieces in the center of the trail.

"What'd I tell you," gulped Chuck.

There was a cut back just ahead, protected by a bit of over-hang. Dex led the way with a rush. Twice more, before they made the shelter of that over-hang, bullets ripped around them venomously. Flattened against the wall, Dex took stock. "Only one answer," he said grimly. "That bunch who split off above the rim to try and draw us onto a false trail must have found out we didn't bite and have come back. And they sighted us from somewhere up there. Well, they can't touch us here."

"No," grunted Wasatch. "But by the same token, we can't touch them."

"I'm not so shore. I'm going to take a look."

Dex laid down his rifle, took the glasses and edged out until he could get a sweep of view back and above. For a time he could see nothing. But presently he caught a shadow of movement away back at one spot where the trail worked around a precipitous shoulder. His glasses steadied. The pygmy figure of a man was there, standing far out on the edge of the trail, waving a serape as though for a signal to the outlaw camp.

"You been champing for a shot at something, Wasatch," rasped Dex over his shoulder. "Here's your chance, but I reckon it'll be only wasted lead."

Wasatch crept out beside him, sighted along Dex's outstretched arm and grunted. "I'll make him quit playing butterfly, anyhow."

He ran up the rear sight of his Winchester and shot from a kneeling position. The snarl of the rifle sent the echoes spinning. "It'll be close," snapped Wasatch.

Dex, his eyes glued to the glasses, caught his breath. He distinctly saw that distant renegade sway as the bullet told. The serape, slipping from paralyzed fingers, fluttered out and down. And then the man spun slowly and toppled outward. Then he was gone like a plummet, a lifeless atom, falling into the gaping depths.

"You damned old wolf," said Dex huskily. "What poison you are with a gun!"

Wasatch smiled mirthlessly. "One more tally for Hop Lee," he said.

And now, welling up from the still distant camp, sounded a thin, long howl of rage. "Sounds like you might have irritated 'em some, Wasatch," grinned Chuck.

"So would you be if a friend of yours took a header for a few thousand feet and lit in your lap," said Wasatch. "Well—let's keep on sliding."

They went on down again, clinging close to the wall. By this time the sun had arched far enough to reach them. The cool blue shadows that had comforted them were gone. Immediately it was hot, for the rocky walls pocketed the heat and laid it all about them.

"I had a hunch to bring one of the canteens when we left the broncs," grumbled Wasatch. "We're liable to be thirsty, before we're done."

Dex said nothing. He was beginning to chafe again. He tried to make an estimate of time—tried to figure that time into miles. "With a little luck," he said— "Dolf ought to have the town boys pretty close to the head of the trail by this time."

Wasatch nodded. "We'll need 'em."

They reached another cut-back where the trail ran out into a wide, secure shelf, yet just beyond it crawled around the base of a sheer pinnacle which jutted out considerably from the main wall. Chuck, in the lead now, started out onto this portion of the trail. Dex caught him by the shoulder.

"Wait a minute, cowboy. Take it just a mite slow. That stretch ahead looks awful damned exposed to me. I been trying to figure why that crowd down at the camp seemed so casual and unworried after their first start of surprise. Maybe that stretch ahead is the answer. Notice how the trail slants out and how narrow it is. I'll bet they can see a man crossing it from down below and I'll bet they've got a dozen guns covering it, right now."

Wasatch nodded. "We'll find out."

Before Dex could stop him, Wasatch darted out onto that ominous stretch of trail, whirled and raced back. He beat a veritable fusillade of lead by scant inches.

Invisible hail ripped along the face of the pinnacle, waist high to an upright man. A cloud of rock dust eddied and bloomed. A few ricochets whimpered upward. The echo of that concerted burst of gun fire boiled through the canyon like brittle thunder.

"You damned old idiot," raved Dex at Wasatch. "That wasn't necessary. They nearly got you."

Wasatch grinned. "We had to find out, didn't we? Well, now we know."

"And having found it out—where does that leave us?" asked Chuck drily.

"Only one answer," growled Dex, still upset by the narrowness of Wasatch's escape. "We don't cross that part of the trail until dark."

"Listen!" snapped Wasatch.

Far up, where the canyon rim swept hazily against the clear blue sky, guns were booming, an indefinably stern and relentless pressure in the steady beat of those reports.

"It's Dolf!" cried Dex. "The old boy is coming through with a lot of good men behind him. They're cleaning out that gang on the trail above us."

"Which means that we may have some coffee colored rats sliding down the trail behind us," growled Wasatch. "Come on, Chuck—we'll make ready for 'em if they show. Dex, you better try another look at the camp. While all this backing and filling is going on, they might be making off with our princess to some other hide out."

Wasatch and Chuck, their rifles ready, worked far

enough out of the switch-back to watch the curve of the trail above, while Dex moved cautiously out to the rim of the ledge, maneuvered a few handy rocks into a blind and brought his glasses into play once more on the canyon below.

He knew immediate satisfaction when he saw the guard still in front of the cabin where Sonia had been placed. But there was no serenity in that camp any longer. They knew down there that some pursuers at least were as close to camp as that exposed portion of the trail and Dex picked up sight of at least a dozen renegades, placed here and there who were watching that portion of trail with ready guns. He saw Jeff Sawtelle, towering above his men as he argued and harangued with a number crowded about him in the open. That new burst of shooting from high up toward the rim was worrying them.

And then Dex saw Don Diego Alviso. The Don was by himself, off to one side, crouched by a corner of a cabin. His attitude was all that of a man sulking and angry. Dex marked this sign with satisfaction. Cross currents of feeling in that outlaw camp was bound to make it more vulnerable.

The shooting from above had thinned out now to an occasional shot. Dex could visualize the set-up. The little group of renegades, driven downward by a contingent of relentless, savage men from above and fearing that at every turn they would make deadly contact with other equally savage, relentless men below, would be like terrified, trapped rats. There was no escape for them. On one side sheer rock, on the other brain paralyzing space and above and below hungry, unerring rifles.

Those renegades would know that there could be no surrender. The temper of these vengeful men who were slowly but surely crushing them between jaws of lead, would be waging a war of extermination, a war to the death.

So was the prophecy of Jeff Sawtelle coming true. Alviso and his gang had committed the crime unpardonable. They had run off with a woman—raided a ranch and taken from it a slim, black-haired girl, whose name had traveled the length and breadth of the range about San Geronimo, clothed in a halo of romance, a girl at whom simple, practical men had looked with awe and respect, for she was a princess!

"Watch yourself, Chuck," came Wasatch's grim warning. "I see two of those pole-cats. See 'em—just past that cut-back. Get set for them. When they make that turn yonder, pour it to 'em. You take the one on the inside, I'll get the other one."

Dex heard the ominous click of gunlocks, as Wasatch and Chuck cocked their rifles. Up above the shooting had ceased entirely. Crouched and terror-stricken the two renegades slithered into view. The crash of the two ready rifles was one report. One of the renegades flopped limply in the trail, face down. The other spun over the edge of the trail, into space.

"Nice work, Chuck," growled Wasatch. "You made a better shot than I did."

"Two more for Hop Lee," said Chuck.

XIII

Dolf Andrews came down the trail on foot, hat pulled low over his bandaged head, eyes burning fiercely in a drawn, pallid face. He took but a single glance at the Mexican lying dead in the trail, then stepped past the body. At sight of Dex and Wasatch and Chuck he tossed high a welcoming hand.

"You galoots had me worried," he croaked. "We run across your broncs up top. Those greasers had 'em. I was afraid they'd burned you down and taken the horses. The boys must have felt like I did, for they shore made quick work of the greasers. Two of 'em got away and came down ahead of us. I see you got one."

Wasatch waved a hand toward the shimmering, sun-drenched space of the canyon. "The other one fell off the trail. Come here and sit down, cowboy. You look plenty seedy."

In single file men came along behind Dolf, nearly a score of them. There was Abe Connors and Bill Kirkle. There was Ben Rellis and Jumbo Dell and the two Edwards boys, Joe and Slim. There was Chick Corcoran and Ed Slade. There were young men and old and at the tail end there was Salty Simmons, sweating and clumsy, but grimly determined.

Dex's heart warmed within him as he looked them over, as he spoke to them and shook their hands. These were men to tie to, men of courage and honor, ready to drop their own affairs and to ride a dangerous, battling trail in the common cause of human decency.

Despite the gravity of what faced them, despite the fact that Sonia was still in the hands of the outlaws and that the future was still one of doubt and danger, Dex had to grin when he faced Salty Simmons. Salty's face was beet-red, his bulging stomach quivering with unaccustomed activity and his eyes rolling every time he considered the depths just beyond the edge of the trail. But there were unmistakable lines about Salty's mouth. Underneath all his fat and clumsiness, Salty was a fighter.

"The railroad will fire you for this, Salty," said Dex.

"Devil take the railroad," puffed Salty. "No bunch of low down pole-cats can steal our princess and get away with it. Me—I'm going to lock my fists in somebody's gullet and separate their lights from their liver for this. That little lady smiled at fat old Salt, and spoke to him kindly. And I'm not forgetting it, by gollies."

"How about it?" asked Dolf. "Is Sonia down there?"

"She's down there. And all right, I'm sure. Alviso and Sawtelle must have had some kind of a row. I was watching through the glasses and I saw Sawtelle knock Alviso down with his fist."

"No sense waiting here," bawled Jumbo Dell. "Let's go on down and get about our rat killing." Jumbo was a big, florid faced puncher with a bull voice. But he would do to ride the river with, any old time.

"Nothing like the present to get at a dirty chore," nodded Abe Connors. "Let's go."

Dex shook his head. He pointed. "See that stretch of

trail ahead? Well, we got about as much chance of crossing that trail in daylight as we have of jumping off and lighting fit to fight. They got better than a dozen guns covering that trail and they'd knock us down like sticks if we tried to cross."

"What'cha aim to do, then?" blurted Salty.

Dex nodded toward the sun, which had arced well toward the west. "That will set, by and by. We wait till dark to cross that open stretch of trail. Might as well sit down and take it easy, boys. There's no sense in trying to rush things and get ourselves all shot to pieces, when by waiting a few hours we can go down with the breaks half way on our side. So far, I believe Sonia to be quite safe. Another thing, we got Sawtelle and Alviso guessing. They've no way of telling how many men are on this trail, for they can't see us from below until we hit that piece of trail ahead. If they knew how many we were they would probably pull out and make a run for it. But they don't want to leave this camp of theirs if they have any chance of standing us off. I think they'll stay put until after dark anyhow, and that will give us the chance we need."

"That's common sense," agreed Abe Connors. "Spread yourselves and take it easy, gents."

"Suits me," gulped Salty, spreading his fat bulk securely on the rocky trail. "Give my hair a chance to settle into place again and my insides maybe will quit jiggling around. Couple of places along this dang fly scratch of a trail I got to thinking and them thoughts shore gave me the unholy jim-jams."

Jumbo Dell grinned. "What were you thinking, Salt?"

"Huh! I was thinking what would happen to a fat geezer like me was I to fall off this trail and tumble about ten miles straight down. I was wondering if I'd pop like a ripe tomater when I hit. And thinking like that shore made me all googly inside. Whoof! This feels good, even if that sun is hot enough to fry aigs."

"I ain't had a chance to ask you about that Varoff jasper," said Dolf. "Did you find any trace of him, Dex?"

"Plenty," nodded Dex grimly. "You know that bald sugar-loaf ridge out northeast of Sunken Wash? Well, we found him up on top of that."

"Not dead?" ejaculated Dolf.

"Dead as a poker. He'd been shot—through the heart. He was killed somewhere else and then carried up and left there on the sugar-loaf."

"Whoever did it wanted him to be found," muttered Dolf thoughtfully. "Buzzards would be sure to circle and anybody coming along the road would be sure and see 'em. Yes sir, whoever killed him wanted him to be found."

"Exactly as I reasoned," Dex nodded. "And there is just one type of mind that would think of such a thing, after murdering a defenseless man. Me—I had no love for Varoff. He was a tin horn and a four-flusher, but I've added his death to the things I'll think of if I can ever get Alviso over the sights of my gun."

"You think Alviso did it?" queried Dolf.

"I'm shore of it. The body was packed up there on the sugar loaf and spread-eagled, face to the sun. No white man would be cruel enough to a dead body to use it that way."

"How were things at the ranch when you left, Dolf?" asked Wasatch.

"Quiet. All the shooting at the time of the raid was lost on Shorty. He was still out but gaining strength. When Milly got back with the gang from town, she had her father with her. I made Jack Duquesne and old man Wright stay at the ranch with Milly. I wouldn't have felt right about leaving her there alone to look after Shorty and Marcia. So Jack and old man Wright agreed to stay with her."

"That was wise," nodded Dex. "With Alviso setting off the spark this way there's no telling what kind of coyotes might drift into the ranch."

The gathering quieted down with stoic patience to wait out the sun. Cigarettes were rolled and pale blue smoke climbed and eddied up the face of the rock. Salty Simmons fell fast asleep, but awoke shortly after with a wild shudder and a strangled gasp.

"What's wrong, Salt?" drawled Slim Edwards. "Swallow your teeth?"

"I was dreaming," wailed Salty.

"You sounded to me like you were choking to death," grinned Slim.

"No sir," affirmed Salty. "I was dreaming. I dreamed I'd slid off'n this gol darned trail and boy—was I doing some tall and fancy tumbling. I kept a falling and a falling and zowie—just as I was about to land on the hardest rocks you ever saw, I woke up. But man, I shore was suffering on the way down."

"You shore sounded like it," said Slim drily.

"Being high up like this always did set my teeth on edge," mumbled Salty. "I got them kind of delicate nerves that won't stand it. Maybe I'm sorta more delicate put together than most folks."

A chuckle ran up and down the line of men. "If a tub of lard is put together delicate, Salt," rumbled Jumbo Dell—"then you shore do qualify."

"If that cussed sun don't get a wiggle on there won't be any lard left in me," complained Salty. "It's frying out of me plumb scandalous."

Dex Sublette understood this byplay, this mild raillery and insult passing between the men. It was their way of killing slow time. But, though they joked and laughed occasionally, Dex knew that in the backs of their minds there was grim menace and cold purpose. They might laugh and joke now, but not a man among them was forgetting the plight of Sonia, nor forgetting the payment they would enact with roaring guns. They were not callous or thoughtless. They merely had an uncomfortable wait ahead of them and they killed time the best way they could.

Dex crawled out to the edge again and made another survey through the glasses. Things were much the same at the outlaw camp. The thing he was most concerned about gave him satisfaction. The guard still stood before the cabin where Sonia was. He wondered what the layout might be closed in against the canyon wall and he edged out a trifle further in an attempt to see. He had the glasses not six inches from his eyes when a terrific force hit them, shattering them and tearing them from his hands. At the same moment, down in the canyon somewhere, a single rifle shot sent the echoes rolling.

Dex scrambled back hurriedly. His face was burning and smarting in a dozen places and his hands felt half paralyzed from the shock. Instantly Wasatch was beside him.

"Did he hit you, kid?"

"No," growled Dex savagely—"but he shot the glasses right out of my hands."

"You're bleeding about the face," snapped Wasatch. "Straighten around and let me look."

"Lead splinters, I guess," growled Dex. "Don't amount to a thing. But a sixty dollar pair of glasses went to hell. With the sun that far over it must have glinted on the lens and some pole-cat made a center shot."

"You're luckier than you know," chided Wasatch. "That spattering lead could have hit your eyes."

"It didn't. Forget it. I'll take the price of those glasses out of somebody's hide—later on."

The incident jerked the men out of their lethargy. After their short battle with the few renegades at the top of the trail, followed by the strain of the trip down the trail, they had known a let-down on finding Dex and Wasatch and Chuck. But that shot had galvanized them anew. They were restlessly grim. They wanted to come to grips with the outlaws, they wanted to start their crusade of smoke and lead against the malignant forces led by Sawtelle and Alviso.

They had heard of the ambush by Alviso that had come so close to costing the lives of Dolf and Shorty. They had seen the crumpled body of little Hop Lee, lying as he had fallen out at the Pinon Ranch. Hardly a man among them but had known little Hop, and had eaten of his cooking. They had liked Hop for his never failing cheerfulness, his wrinkled slant-eyed grin. And above all was the fact that Alviso and his range thugs had stolen the slim, lovely boss of the ranch.

Stern and unimaginative as these men were, there had been an aura of mystery and charm and romance about the coming of a foreign princess to the Pinon Ranch, which had turned the thoughts of these men inward, to the memory of vague, half forgotten ideals which had warmed and colored their hard, practical lives. By even the touch of his hand, Don Diego Alviso had besmirched those ideals and there was but one answer for that in the hearts of these men.

"Damn that sun," growled Chick Corcoran.

It seemed to move with maddening slowness, yet Dex, as he glanced upward at Chick's word, saw that it was appreciably closer to the crest of the Thunderheads than when last he looked at it. Across the canyon shadows were forming, blue and remote as yet, but chafing at the bonds of slanting sunlight like the waters of some strange and mystic sea.

194

"If," said Salty—"I could kinda get myself all in one chunk again, I could sort of admire this scenery. Look at them colors, will you. They're throwed together plumb careless like, but they sort of flatten you out, don't they?"

"You talk in the damndest circles," growled Jumbo Dell. "Right now, if you're flattened out, Salt—then a bull-frawg ain't no thicker than a postage stamp."

"Aw—you're just dumb," sniffed Salty. "You don't even know what I mean."

"How could I," Jumbo retorted—"when you don't know yourself?"

"That sun," grumbled Chick Corcoran—"ain't moved a bit in the last half hour. I know, cause I been watching it."

"It must have moved," argued Salty. "Time fugits, you know."

"Time—what?"

"Fugits—fugits."

Chick looked at Jumbo. "He's got it. There's only one thing to do, Jumbo."

"That's right," rumbled Jumbo. "I've heard it said that hot sun gives some men hydrophoby. Before Salt starts biting some of us, we better chuck him off the trail. What say?"

Salty's eyes rolled and he shuddered. He said no more.

The sun was finally gone, sinking into a sea of scarlet and burnished gold beyond the violet bulk of the Thunderheads. A stir ran through the waiting men.

Wasatch rolled one more cigarette.

"Those hombres must know we been waiting for darkness to get across that piece of exposed trail, Dex," he said. "And they ain't going to be caught sound asleep or by surprise. They aim to bottle us up somewhere along the trail further down."

Dex nodded. "I been thinking of that. Yet, there isn't a thing we can do but gamble. I'm going ahead, so if there is trouble waiting, you boys will be warned when I bump into it."

"You're wrong in one thing," grunted Wasatch. "I'm going first. Don't argue—I'm going first."

"I'll meet you half way," shrugged Dex. "We'll go together."

With the sun gone, twilight rolled up out of the canyon in thickening waves. The lower reaches of the canyon were already dark, but the after-glow of sunset spread its mocking light along the east wall, fretting the men in its reluctance to depart.

Dex turned to the men. "We don't want to go at this thing without any system," he said. "There's a trail that leads north up the canyon, close in below this wall. Whether there is a getaway trail to the south, I don't know. I doubt it. Anyway, here's how we'll tackle the proposition. When we hit the bottom I want you, Dolf, to take Ben and Jumbo, Joe and Slim, and block that trail to the north. Wasatch and I will cut straight for the cabin where Sonia is. Abe, you take the rest of the boys and cut your way right through the camp. That gang down below are going to have a certain edge on us.

They know the layout down there and we don't. But, unless they have got a getaway laid out to the south, we'll have 'em pretty well pocketed."

"It's dark enough," said Wasatch. "Let's go."

With Dex and Wasatch in the lead they moved out across that dangerous bit of trail. Dex held his breath, expecting any moment to hear the crash of gun fire and have hungry lead cutting around them. But down in the canyon all was still, except for the far off song of the river, which seemed to deepen in tone under the masking darkness.

It was particularly eerie, traveling that trail in the darkness. On their right hand was the security of the wall, on their left nothing but black, empty space.

"Salty," muttered Wasatch—"I'll bet he scratches his clothes off, rubbing against this wall."

Bootheels grated, spur rowels tinkled, yet these sounds were absorbed and muffled by the immense sponge of space. For all practical purposes, their progress was virtually noiseless.

They moved through two more cut-backs, then followed a single long slant downward. Somehow, Dex could tell that they were not far from the bottom now. He could feel it. That space out to his left did not draw at a man like it had before. Queer, how you could sense those things.

Dex grabbed Wasatch by the arm and stopped him. Down there in the Stygian gloom a match had flared for a moment, then flickered out. A thread of caution ran back along the line of men. They stilled, breathless and listening. Dex's nostrils wrinkled. The air was moving upward and it brought to him the scent of tobacco smoke.

Dex tightened his fingers on Wasatch's arm. He sensed, rather than saw Wasatch nod. They went forward with infinite caution. Behind them Salty Simmons' face was contorted. He had wrapped one fat arm about his mouth and nose, he was gagging and choking. It was heroic effort, but it didn't work. A strangled, choking sneeze, too long held back, shook Salty like a tempest.

In that straining silence it was akin to a full throated shout. Below, where that match had flared, sounded an exclamation of alarm. A curse, an involuntary challenge, and then the crimson flare of gun flame and the roar of report, to break that brooding canyon night wide open.

XIV

With that first burst of gunfire, high up on the canyon rim, Sonia watched a small panic sweep over the outlaw camp. For a moment it seemed, she was forgotten. Men swarmed into view forming in the open, staring up at those far, dim heights. Sawtelle, roaring like a bull, raged back and forth among them, arguing, cursing, trying to still his own fears and those of his men. Don Diego Alviso, dark and malignant, kept apart from Sawtelle, as though fearing the wrath of the giant outlaw chief. And Sonia, as she watched and listened, realized that despite their swagger, their bluster and hard brutality, these men were all obsessed by a common fear—the fear of retribution for their various misdeeds, catching up with them.

But when that shooting up on the rim died out and no more sounded, they quieted and, as though ashamed of their momentary show of panic, became matter-of-fact and carelessly insouciant once more.

Sawtelle's wild bellows softened to his usual rumble and he began giving concise orders. Sonia saw men get rifles from the various cabins and take up posts of guarding and defense. She stood in the doorway and looked up along that sheer, towering wall. Nowhere up there could she see any sign of movement. In fact, from this point, it seemed unbelievable that there was a trail down that wall, except for one place, well toward the bottom where the trail cut around the base of a pinnacle in such a way that some forty or fifty yards of it was visible. She heard Sawtelle order a number of his men to station themselves with ready guns and watch that section of trail.

She saw Alviso, now feeling that the first torrent of Sawtelle's rage had gone, go up and speak to Sawtelle. And she heard Sawtelle curse and saw him, with one lethal blow of his fist, knock Alviso sprawling. Then the outlaw chief rocked away, growling more instructions to the remainder of his men.

Sonia saw Alviso drag himself to unsteady feet and, even at the distance, the expression on his face made her shudder. Never had she glimpsed such black, poisonous rage and hate mirrored on a man's face. Alviso's mouth was bleeding from the effects of Sawtelle's blow and he wiped at it with the tail of his silken neckerchief.

And now she saw an old, white bearded man with a crooked leg come shambling toward her prison. Under one arm he carried a roll of blankets, in his free hand a bucket of water. Following him came a renegade with a rifle.

It was natural to expect a certain mellowing from the years, a kindliness in a man of the evident age of this old fellow with the blankets and water, but as he reached the cabin his voice spat out at Sonia with savage senility.

"Git back in that cabin and stay there. Git away from that door, you brash hussy. If the boss was wise he'd cut yore throat and throw you in the river. Never was a woman but brought trouble with 'em. Here's some blankets and water, but I'll be damned if I stand for bein' made regular nurse maid to such as you."

Sonia said nothing. She was shocked and bewildered. She had not asked to come to such a place as this. She had been carried here ruthlessly and her mere presence was a signal for savage hate from these godless men. The old renegade went out and the man who had accompanied him with the rifle slammed the door, fastened it from the outside. Sonia heard the old man speak to him.

"Things are comin' to a hell of a pass when we got to watch over a damned woman, Wash."

"Was I the chief, I'd cut Alviso's heart out for this," growled the guard in answer. "For years we've had this snug hide-out. Now we'll have hell on wheels on our trail. And all because of a pretty face. I tell you, Shag—I've been against Alviso and his greaser friends all the way along. I told the boss that over a month ago. You can't depend on greasers. They lose their heads and go spooky too easy. Do you think Jeff is figuring on pulling out?"

"Not unless he has to. This camp is too handy, too well placed to give it up unless there's no other out. I reckon he'll wait and see how things work out."

The sound of voices ceased and Sonia went slowly back to the bunk. She spread the blankets there, sipped a little water from her cupped hands, then curled up to rest.

She was amazed at her own composure. Here was cause enough for literal heart-break, for despair. The Sonia of a month ago might have given way before the stark realization of her predicament. But the Sonia of the moment was cool and self-possessed. Much could happen in the next few hours. Wisely she concluded to let her thoughts dwell on possible rescue than upon dreary hopelessness. That distant outburst of firing told that men were on the trail. Among those men would be Dexter Sublette, that tawny headed foreman of hers—that lean, brown, cold jawed rider, whose personality had begun to affect her life so strangely.

Thought of him warmed and invigorated her, made her eyes wide and dreamy. Back through the years of her life she had met many men, of all stations of life. Yet, all of them, emperors, princes, royalty of all kinds, statesmen and courtiers, paled and shrunk in stature beside this lean, hardy son of the western ranges, Dexter Sublette.

The slow hours wheeled past. Once there came a single, ringing report, high up the cliff and it was followed by a howl of rage from the outlaws scattered about, outside. She did not know that these outlaws had seen the lifeless body of one of Alviso's renegade vaqueros catapult through sickening space and crash horridly at the base of the cliff. But that howl of anger told her one thing. It told her that the original burst of firing had not stopped the men who were riding on the trail of rescue.

Midday came and passed. Pangs of hunger made itself felt. And then the door of her prison was opened and the old savage outlaw was there again, bearing a rude platter of food. He snarled at her wordlessly as he put it down and backed out. The food was coarse, but savory and Sonia ate hungrily.

After her meal she lay down again and dozed for a time. A new burst of firing from high up the rim jerked her wide awake once more. This also was soon done with, but not long after two shots, very close together, rang out much closer in. And then not long after there was still another report.

She heard her guard call restlessly to someone, but the answer was far enough away to be indistinct. Later, she heard Sawtelle roaring at some of his men.

"Watch that open stretch of the trail. Don't let anybody by, or your souls will roast in hell. Don't go to sleep on the job."

This meant but one thing. Those men who had taken the vengeance trail were closing in, slowly but surely. She closed her eyes again and it seemed that she could see them, grim and intent and savage, working down that giddy trail, closing in, closing in. And in the lead there would be Dexter Sublette, indomitable and terribly certain in his argosy of retribution.

Then, as the long afternoon slid away without further sound or interruption, she guessed at the strategy of Dex and his men. They were waiting for darkness—the friendly cover of shadows which would hide their final dash for the bottom. She wondered at the fact of Sawtelle standing his ground. Either the outlaw chief believed that the attackers lacked numbers to carry the camp by assault, or he was planning some murderous trap for them. Fear came back to Sonia, not for herself, but for those staunch men who were moving to her rescue. She visualized the price they might pay for this—the cost in blood and death and she shuddered. And what for? For her—one lone woman in a world of women.

Indirectly, behind it all, she saw that she was largely at fault. Against the quiet advice of Dexter Sublette she had, in a way encouraged the advances of Don Diego. Had she listened to Dex, on that very first day when they had ridden down to the crest of the great sage slope and met Alviso and his men while returning, perhaps this thing could not have happened. And then, on that terrible day when she had wielded a quirt in her stormy anger on the very man who would have protected her— She had, in her pique, agreed to ride with Alviso and had quirted Dex Sublette when he refused to let her go. And Dex had not taken his wrath out on her. Under the fury of it he had thrashed Alviso savagely and set at work the train of vicious circumstances which had led up to that final raid. And still, despite all that, Dex was faithful. Somehow she was certain he was up there on that trail, waiting his chance to drive through to her rescue. Her heart told her that. And it told her other things which set her lips to quivering and her eyes to misting. And now, for the first time since the raid on the Pinon Ranch, she gave way to tears. She cried silently, scourged with self-abasement.

It grew cooler and the interior of her prison thickened with gloom. The sun had set. The afternoon was gone and the canyon was filling with mists and shadows. She sat up and dried her tears. There was a tension growing in the outlaw camp. Sonia could feel it herself. It came in through the walls of her prison and put savage life into the stillness and the waiting.

The light faded rapidly. Soon it was so dark Sonia could no longer see the walls of her cabin. And in that blackness she prowled about, restless, on edge— waiting, waiting. . . .

The silence of the night was blown into fragments by the rip and roar of shots, close in, low down—at the bottom of the trail. A single long, wavering cry of warning rang out. And then all voices, all other sounds, were smothered and drowned under the thundering cacophony of gun-fire.

Sonia stumbled to one of the cabin walls and through a narrow crack formed by the shrinking of the logs as they had dried, tried to get some picture of what was taking place out there in the night. Only one thing could she see, and that was the crimson lick and flash of gun-flame. There was no let down in the shooting. It was savage and concerted and steady.

And now she heard a voice—the great roaring shout of Sawtelle, the outlaw chief. It was caught up and carried along by the shrill yammering of other outlaw voices and it seemed she could glimpse men racing past her prison, scrambling uncouth shapes outlined against the flare of the guns. She could visualize Sawtelle, the startling size of him, his clumsy, crushing, brutal strength, his mad, feral rage.

There was no answer to the howl of the outlaws. Only it seemed that the rumble and crash of gun-fire rose to a greater intensity. Invisible blows struck the walls of her prison—lead, winging across the night, missing human flesh, but finding a billet in the cabin logs.

It seemed that the shooting was drawing closer to the cabin and she heard Sawtelle roaring again and this time there was a new note in his voice—a note of uncertainty, of desperation.

There could be but one answer to that, reasoned Sonia. The outlaws were being driven back. A wild gust of pride caught her up. That attacking force was wasting no time in aimless yelling or shouting. They were fighting silently, but with a ferocity and power that was driving the outlaws back. Dex Sublette would be out there, a still, bleak fury, his guns exacting a terrible toll from the despoilers. And from the sound of the shooting there would be many men behind him, grim, indomitable fellows who had rallied unselfishly to the cause. They were fighting for her!

So close at hand that it chilled her blood, a man screamed in death agony. She heard a dull, muffled thump, as though he had fallen back against the cabin wall. She wondered if this could be her guard.

Now there was someone fumbling at her door. Dex! It must be Dex!

She flew to the door, her heart swelling with emotion. It would be like Dex, to come straight to her through all that hell of battle. And Sonia knew what her greeting to him would be—her arms—her lips—for this man—this man—

The door crashed open. Through it charged a gigantic bulk. Sonia went cold with terror. Her senses were inordinately sharpened. Even though it was dark it seemed that she could see and her instinct of recognition was true. This was not Dex Sublette. This was Sawtelle.

His voice held the harsh growling note of a savage animal. "Where are you—where are you?"

Sonia shrank back, slithering lightly to the far corner of the cabin. Somehow he heard her and he came blundering that way, his great hands pawing and reaching. Twice Sonia ducked away from him but always he followed, like some insensate, blundering juggernaut.

Now there was a third person in the room and a voice, thin and vicious and gutturally sibilant, cut across Sonia's consciousness.

"Sawtelle! We even it all now, Senor."

The room flickered ominously crimson before the lick and slash of gun flame, and the thunder of the shots was like the crushing impact of huge hammers in Sonia's brain.

She heard Sawtelle gasp and choke. Then he also was shooting. Crouched low against a side wall, Sonia watched with wide and horrified eyes while the two outlaw leaders shot it out. The gun flame was like jagged lightning cutting across the blackness. And in the broken flare of it she saw Sawtelle and she saw Don Diego Alviso. They were like distorted figments of nightmare, drawn from some infernal pit and thrown into this small room to blast lightning and thunder at each other.

Alviso was crouched, low and compact. But Sawtelle was weaving from side to side, like a fighter caught in a fury of blows which could not drop him but which kept him off balance, on his heels. His voice lifted again, but there was no coherence, nothing intelligible in his cry. It was a steady, unbroken roar, hoarser and thicker and choked.

Sawtelle stumbled and went to his knees. There was a terrible, strained intensity to his cry now, like a man being swept toward a pit of everlasting blackness and unable to retreat. Suddenly his great, bony head jerked gruesomely backward, his cry broke off and he crashed down. It was like the final fall of some great, mortally wounded beast.

The thunder of the shots ceased and there was no more gun lightning to sear the brain. But there was something leaping through the blackness.

Before Sonia could retreat or move, hands settled upon her, hands which bit into her soft flesh like the talons of some ghoulish bird. Instinctively Sonia fought back, but her strength was as nothing against the savageness of Alviso. He dragged her toward the door. She opened her mouth to scream and it seemed that he sensed her thought. For he struck a short, hooking blow with his clenched fist.

Sharp agony followed that blow, agony like a needle of flame through Sonia's brain. And then everything whirled out into nothingness and a gulf of merciful shadows seemed to swallow her up.

Panting and snarling through set teeth, Alviso swept up the senseless girl and jack-knifed her across his shoulder. Holding her there with one hand, he drew a gun with the other and stumbled from the door.

Out there the battle was still raging, but Alviso could tell that the outlaws were being driven back, that they were breaking on all sides. He swung about the corner of the cabin and ran, back toward the main heart of the canyon. There, with the blackness laying a protecting blanket all about him, he turned north.

He slowed his pace now, moving cautiously. His head twisted to one side, he marked the most northern limits of the fight, for he could tell it by the flicker of the guns. And he circled those limits with the unconscious cunning of a creeping panther.

He was beyond the limits of the flat where the camp was built, now. To his left the earth was beginning to slant steeply, so he bore more directly in toward the east wall, driving his laboring muscles to the task of fighting that growing slope.

His eyes, burning red, stabbed the blackness before him. His senses strained to call him a warning if there were any men ahead of him. But the blackness flowed past him, empty and unmenacing. And of a sudden his feet struck what he had been working toward, that narrow trail which ran due north, close against the base of the eastern wall.

A low mutter of savage satisfaction broke through the uneven cadence of his panting breath and he fled along that trail into the protecting silence and blackness of the upper canyon.

XV

That unfortunate sneeze, which had broken so treacherously from Salty Simmons, was the fuse to an inferno. Yet Dex Sublette welcomed the break. The tension which had built up and grown throughout those long afternoon hours, had cracked wide open, now. Here at last was action—here something definite to strike at, to loose the fury of his purpose on. He went down those last few yards of trail in a berserk charge, straight into the flaming guns of the renegades who guarded it.

Automatically, Dex was shooting and close behind his shoulder was the whimpering snarl of old Wasatch, eager for the fray. If there was lead whistling about Dex's ears, he did not hear it. His fury was still and silent and terrific. He crashed into a twisting cursing figure and literally shot the man out of his way.

The sheer, pure impetuousness of Dex and his men, rolled like a tidal wave over the renegades grouped at the bottom of the trail. The cowboys and the men from San Geronimo shot their way into the clear with a savagery which the outlaws could not match. Yet here was only the beginning. Renegades came swarming and the night was a madness of flame and lead and death. A stride behind Dex and Wasatch, Chick Corcoran reared suddenly on his toes and pitched forward on his face, Chick, one of the most eager to be at the work of retribution, had ridden his last trail.

Back further in that charging group Bill Kirkle cursed savagely as his right leg was jerked from under him and he went down, that leg twisted and broken by the slug that had crashed into it. Almost at Kirkle's side another man went down, a curly headed young puncher who had happened to be in San Geronimo when Milly Duquesne had brought word of the raid and had jumped to do his part in call for men. He writhed and twisted there on the ground for a moment or two, moaned softly, then lay limp and still.

Out in front Wasatch caught Dex by the shoulder and drove him to the ground. "Stay low, kid—stay low," he gritted harshly in Dex's ear. "In the dark most shots go high. Keep under 'em."

Going forward in diving rushes, Dex drove ahead. He had placed as nearly as he could the position of the cabin in which Sonia had been imprisoned, and he was driving for it. Close beside him, Wasatch was fighting, as a grizzled wolf, old and experienced, would fight. Every move the old rider made was a telling one. He shot regularly, but not wildly. Each time Wasatch pulled a trigger it was just below and to one side of a gun flash. And renegades were dying out in front of him, cut down by lead from an old tiger whose deadliness in the dark was uncanny.

The outlaws fought stubbornly, but it was obvious that the numbers attacking them was a surprise. Here was power and force much greater than they had anticipated and a thread of panic ran through the renegades. They began giving back until the roaring voice of Sawtelle cursed and exhorted them.

But of what use curses and exhortations when a line of livid death poured at them with ever rising pressure and certainty. And, desperate as the outlaws were, they had not the purpose behind them as did this relentless group of attackers. And, even though the stage for surprise had been cleverly set by the renegades, they themselves were the victims of the real surprise for they had not dreamed that such numbers or such ferocity would roll out of the night to attack.

The tide was setting heavily against the renegades now, for Dex and his companions had located the foe fully and were lacing the night with lead. The return fire was becoming sporadic and wild and the attacks began sweeping farther and farther out across the flat toward the cabins.

Dex fought like an automaton, driving forward, driving forward. He knew his guns were empty when they would no longer leap in recoil and he reloaded them subconsciously, for his staring, searching eyes were always fixed out there—where that cabin ought to be.

"We got 'em licked," panted Wasatch in his ear. "We got 'em licked, kid. They're breaking everywhere."

It seemed to Dex that right after Wasatch spoke, he heard a burst of firing which he could identify above the rest of the shooting, because it had a heavy, muffled note to it, as though it had taken place behind walls or in some deep cavern. And as a half covered overtone to it there was a hoarse, savage roaring, like the sound of an imprisoned animal.

But a grunt and a curse from Wasatch brought him back to the events close beside him. Dex whirled, but could not find Wasatch.

"Wasatch!" he yelled. "Where—?"

"Down here, kid—in back of you. They got me through the leg. Busted. I'll be all right. Go on ahead. I'll still cause 'em trouble from here."

Dex bored on alone. There was not much resistance now. It was breaking up rapidly. Abe Connors, with fighting men at his back, was doing his part of the job as Dex had outlined it to him, back up there on the trail. Abe was hammering the renegades back and back toward the south end of the flat.

Now Dex sensed the dim bulk of a cabin before him. Was it the right one? He darted forward and stumbled over a dead man lying before the open door. Dex plunged through that door. "Sonia!" he called hoarsely. "Sonia!"

There was no move, no answer. Dex coughed. The interior of that cabin was thick and acrid with powder fumes. Dex found a match, scratched it alight. The flame was too feeble at first to pierce the gloom, but as it licked higher it threw a pallid half light through the small room.

Dex saw something on the floor, something huge and sprawled and still. The match went out. Dex lit another, moved a stride or two and bent over. There, staring up at him, eyes rolled back and sightless, was the repulsive, bony face of Jeff Sawtelle. Dex knew it was Sawtelle, though he had never met the man face to face before. Other men who had, had told him of the huge, gross, clumsy bulk, of the frog-like eyes, the great beaked nose. Yes, this was Sawtelle. And he was dead, literally shot to pieces. The second match went out.

A cold, dread premonition was gripping Dex's heart. There could be but one answer to this dead man. Someone in his own organization had done this to him—had shot him down. But who—and why?

Alviso! That would be it—Alviso! And the reason? "Sonia!" whispered Dex hoarsely. "If that damned greaser—"

He whirled and charged out of the cabin. Only in an abstract sort of way did he realize that the fight was about over with. The shooting had thinned out, all but a few casual shots down at the southern end of the flat. And Jumbo Dell was bellowing the fact that—"We've cleaned the damned rats out, boys—we've cleaned 'em out!"

Dex knifed a savage way through the night, heading up canyon. He lifted his voice in a hoarse, ringing shout. "Dolf! Oh—Dolf!"

The answer came, out there ahead. Dex bumped into Dolf and Joe and Slim Edwards. Joe was holding Slim up, who was torn with the pain of a smashed shoulder. "What's wrong, Dex?" cried Dolf.

"Anybody get by you boys on that north trail?" Dex's voice sounded dry and thin and unnatural.

"Not a damned one. Two or three tried it, but we discouraged 'em—quick!"

"Be shore of that, for Gawd's sake. I can't find Sonia and from the layout of things in the cabin where she was—Sawtelle and somebody must have fought it out for her. Sawtelle is in there—dead. But Sonia's gone."

"You think—Alviso?"

"If we cain't locate him—it must be. We got to get lights. There must be lanterns or candles around here somewhere."

"Rats don't come back after a fire," growled Dolf.

"Have the boys touch off this damned camp. You'll have light enough then, to look over this flat."

Someone was shouting for Dex, down at the south end. It was Abe Connors. When Dex reached him, Abe shot a terse question at him. "The girl—did you find her?"

"Not yet. I'm afraid Alviso has given us the slip—and taken her with him. We got to have light here, Abe—so we can get some idea of who is down and who ain't. Have the boys go through the cabins, make sure the joints are empty, then touch 'em off."

Abe went off, shouting. Dex, his mind cold and dazed, went back and searched and called until he found Wasatch. The old rider was profanely grim. He was binding up his own wounded leg as best he could in the blackness.

"Sonia," croaked Dex. "I can't find her, Wasatch. I got a feeling—I got a cold, hungry hunch that Alviso has out-timed us." He told Wasatch about Sawtelle, lying dead in the cabin where Sonia had been. "There was only one man in this camp who would have shot it out with Sawtelle like that. Alviso, Wasatch—and he's gone—taking Sonia with him."

Dex was broken and desperate. Wasatch gripped his arm. "Hang on to yourself, kid. Let's think. If Alviso has got her, which way would he go?"

"He couldn't have taken the north trail for Dolf and the Edwards boys were guarding it. Maybe he went south—maybe there's a way south that we don't know of."

"Don't think so," growled Wasatch. "If there had been a lot of those outlaw whelps would have run for it instead of staying and fighting it out the way they did. Me, I been in too many gun brawls not to sense when the other side has got their tails up, when they're in a panic. And tonight the coyote blood was running strong. They'd have broke and run for it early, if there was anywhere for them to run to. But we were pretty much between them and that north trail—so they fought, because there was no other out for them. It's possible, you know, that Alviso might have made a circle that took him around Dolf and onto that north trail. I'd check on that, was I you."

A gust of acrid smoke came drifting across the flat. "What's up?" demanded Wasatch.

"We're burning this camp. Here, I'm getting you over to where some of the boys can look after you."

Dex lifted Wasatch until he could balance on his sound leg, then put an arm about him and half carried him over to where Abe Connors was supervising the firing of the cabins. Already there were crimson tongues of flame licking up inside of the doomed buildings. The only ones to be spared were two small feed sheds close to the corrals, where the horses were.

The victors, now that the fight was over, moved efficiently about and as the stygian darkness fled before the mounting glare of the burning buildings, began a careful check-up of the casualties. Grimly and gently the bodies of Chick Corcoran and the curly headed youngster were carried in and put down. Two men brought Bill Kirkle, his leg hanging limp, between them.

Jumbo Dell came in alone, a dead men cradled in his big arms. Jumbo's face was stony, but his eyes were frankly wet. The dead man was Ben Rellis. He and Jumbo had been side-kicks for a long time.

Wasatch, Bill Kirkle and Slim Edwards were made to lie down on wads of blankets, which Abe Connors had thoughtfully removed from the cabins before firing them. Their wounds were roughly bandaged. There were only two wounded outlaws found and both of these were dying. The outlaw dead were left as they fell.

One of those dying outlaws was conscious. Dex bent over him. "You haven't got a chance," said Dex. "But before you go you can half way square accounts. Is there any other trail out of here except to the north and up the east wall?"

The outlaw shook his head. "I got nothin' to say," he mumbled harshly.

"I'm looking for Alviso, you know," argued Dex. "He killed Sawtelle."

The outlaw's eyes flickered. "You're lyin'," he charged.

"No—I'm not. I found Sawtelle. He was in the cabin where Sonia—Miss Stephens had been held. Sawtelle was all shot to pieces—dead when I got there. None of my gang got him. I was the first to get into the cabin. But there he was—dead. The girl—was gone. And we haven't been able to find Alviso."

"That damned greaser!" The outlaw choked and coughed, shaking all over. "If I thought—he did for Jeff," he panted weakly.

"There's no other answer," argued Dex. "I wouldn't lie to a dying man."

The outlaw nodded slowly. "If Jeff is dead—I can't hurt anybody—but Alviso. Yeah—there is a way out, to the south. But that trail coming in from on top is a wide, level road alongside of it. Some of our boys made a break for that trail. One or two might get over it—the rest won't. I know—I tried it myself one time and gave up. Jeff—had been over it. But he was strong—like a gorilla. His hands were like steel hooks. He could hang on where—other men couldn't. Me—I don't think—Alviso would have nerve—enough to—try it."

"And," said Dolf, who had been listening in beside Dex—"he wouldn't be able to take Sonia over it. Dex—that damned greaser is around here somewhere. I'll bet—"

Dolf broke off—staring. Into the circle of light staggered a fat, familiar figure. It was Salty Simmons. But Salty's hands were pressed tight against his body and his face was a pallid mask of desperation and agony. He collapsed suddenly.

Dex ran to him. Salty was shot through the body. The creeping pallor of his face told its own story. "Water—quick, somebody," cried Dex.

Salty shook his head. "No use. Done for and know it. Dex—listen. Alviso—gone north. Saw him—I saw

218

him. He—had our Princess—over—his shoulder. He—was circlin'—wide—to get above Dolf—and other boys. I was down then—this bullet. Wanted to yell. Couldn't. Lost my gun—couldn't shoot. But I crawled an' staggered—an' got here—somehow. Wanted—you to know—Dex. Go—get him. Go—get—him. Tell—little lady—old Salt—"

Salty collapsed like a sack. He seemed to shrink as the life went out of him.

Dex stood up. His face was old and bleak and stony. Men—good men—old friends, dead and dying about him. Salty, with his last words had given the reason. The little lady, he had called her. And Alviso had gone north—taking her with him.

Dex whirled. "Give me a rifle—somebody." A Winchester was shoved into his hands. Chuck moved up beside him. "Come on, Dex," he said gravely. "You and me'll take this trail—to a finish."

XVI

They moved away from the glare of the burning buildings and out into the blackness of the upper canyon. They found the trail and went along it. But that trail was narrow and hard to follow in its unfamiliarity. Yet they went ahead, feeling it out, testing it with each step. For a time they seemed utterly blind, until, removed from the glare, their eyes began adjusting to the darkness. Then their pace grew more rapid.

Dex's brain, numbed by the staggering cost of the

attack, functioned automatically and mechanically. It told him that Alviso would not be able to travel very fast, carrying the burden of Sonia. Yet there were a thousand pockets of blackness in which he might crouch and let them go by. The uncertainty of it was maddening. At any step they might be met with lead. All the odds were against them—everything in favor of Alviso. But there was only one thing to do and that was to go on.

For a time the trail was fairly level, winding its way along between sandstone boulders that had at one time been part of the east wall, but, through the ages, by the agency of rain and frost, wind and heat, had weathered from the parent wall and plunged down to a resting place below.

Perhaps a quarter of a mile of this endured before the trail tipped slowly upward, writhing up the wall at a long slant. Here, magically enough, the light increased. It was as though the stars were unable to pierce the heart of the canyon, but up here along the wall their light laid a dim, silvery effulgence. Dex and Chuck increased their pace almost to a run until their breath rasped harshly in their throats and the sweat coursed down them.

They stopped, as though by mutual consent, to listen. For a time their ears were muffled by the pounding of their hearts and the whistle of hard won breath. Then, somewhere out ahead of them came a faint metallic sound, the clink of metal on rock. A spur rowel, perhaps.

"He's—up ahead, Dex," muttered Chuck.

Again they poured their desperate strength against the slope and as they climbed, the sensation of space grew out on their left—space and height. Above them the wall of the canyon loomed, a mocking wall, washed by the silver of the stars. Below them lay gloom.

They stopped to listen once more. And now, faint but certain they could hear the gasping breath of a man engaged in mortal physical strain. It was as Dex had gambled, the strain of carrying Sonia was exhausting Alviso. They were gaining rapidly.

Dex grew insensible to his own physical limits. He drove at the slope like a madman and grimly Chuck stuck to his heels.

Here the trail swung outward, around a ragged shoulder, which bulged like some ungainly growth from the canyon wall. Little more than twenty feet above the trail the point of that bulging rockface protruded, yet where the trail skirted it, one seemed balanced on the brink of all eternity. And as Dex writhed his way around it he marveled that any man could have made it, carrying a person with him.

Now cold horror shook Dex. Perhaps Sonia was not out there ahead, with Alviso. Perhaps her slim body lay far below, crushed and mangled on the cruel rocks below. Perhaps they had already passed her.

He shook his head wildly. That could not be. After all the sacrifice, all the terrific, battling efforts—

"Back!"

The word hissed out of the darkness of the pocket beyond the bulging rockface. "Back! Another step and you lose everything!"

It was difficult to recognize the voice of Alviso. It sounded thick and clotted and tortured—the voice of a man who had driven himself to the limit of his strength and was racked with desperate purpose and resolve. Dex was dead still and he did not answer.

"You do not fool me," came Alviso's words. "I have heard you behind me. I know you are there. And you must listen carefully. You can not reach me with lead, for the angle protects me. But I am exhausted. I can go no further. Yet, should you come for me, I still have the strength to push that which I have with me—off the trail. And if that should happen, what would it win you to kill me? You understand my meaning?"

Dex twisted around, pressed his lips close to Chuck's ear. "Talk to him," he murmured. "Talk to him. Make him think you are alone. Don't let him know that I am here. Talk to him."

Chuck cleared his throat. "I hear you, Alviso. You—you seem to hold high cards. I'm willing to bargain with you. What is your price?"

"Who is that?" asked Alviso.

"This is Rollins—Chuck Rollins."

"And who is with you?"

"Nobody is with me. I'm alone."

"You lie. I heard you following, far back along the trail. There was more than one—then."

"That was Sublette, down there," said Chuck. "But

he was packing lead—wounded. And he played out, back along the trail. I came on alone."

There was silence. "And you wish to bargain with me, eh?" When Alviso's voice came again it was taunting, some of its old arrogance showing again. "Perhaps it is too late to bargain with me."

Chuck made his tone almost humble. "I'm hoping not. If you'll just let us have Miss Sonia back—you can name your own price."

All the time this talk was going on, Dex Sublette had been frantically busy. With infinite caution he had squatted and drawn off both boots. He laid these on the trail, then unbuckled and laid his chaps beside them. To this pile he added his rifle. Then he literally crawled between Chuck's feet. He stood up in back of Chuck, leaned over and put his lips to Chuck's ear once more.

"Keep talking. Hold him there, somehow."

Chuck nodded. "How about it, Alviso? Are you willing to listen to reason?"

Alviso laughed, and there was almost an unbalanced quality in that laugh. "The proud gringos would come on their knees to me now, eh? On their knees to me, Don Diego Alviso. They do not shout their stupid boasts or curse at me now. They whine and they crawl. I find humor in that, gringo dog."

"I'll crawl if I have to," said Chuck. "Like I said, you can write your own ticket. Only give me back our boss."

All the feral cruelty in the Spaniard's make-up showed now. "You do not like the thought, eh—the thought of the proud lady falling to those hungry rocks below? But how easy it would be for me to send her there. She is here beside me, and her wrists and her feet are tied together and there is cloth across her lips. She could not even scream as she fell. A pleasant thought, eh gringo? To be bound and helpless and falling—falling—with nothing below but the hungry rocks. Think of it, gringo—for that is what will happen if the thought should come to me strongly enough. I will play with that thought now."

Chuck twisted, looked behind him. His breath went out in a low, strangled gasp. Dex Sublette was not on the trail. Instead, limned against the faint star glow, he was clinging to that bulging rockface, not unlike a huge lizard. Even as Chuck watched, Dex inched himself a little higher.

Chuck's blood seemed to curdle in his veins. How could a man cling to that rock—and climb it? It did not seem credible. It was inhuman. Yet Dex Sublette at that moment was inhuman. He was going up that rock, his body fairly hanging over sheer space. If he slipped—!

The cold sweat started all over Chuck. He knew what Dex's desperate plan was. If he could gain the top of that rock bulge, he would be crouched over Alviso. And from there, by leap or shot, he might attack successfully. But the incredible wonder of it was that he should be able to cling to that sheer shoulder of rock. Chuck tore his eyes. from Dex and began to talk again, a little wildly.

"Listen, Alviso—don't talk like that. What would it gain you to kill a helpless girl? There must be something else—some reward you would consider. Your personal freedom—range, land, cattle—whatever your price is, it'll be paid."

Alviso laughed again. "It amuses me—all this shooting and killing—this battle over one mere woman. I laugh at myself that I should have gambled so much for so little. And Sawtelle—sh—I must tell you about Sawtelle. What a clumsy fool he was! The girl set him against me and, stupid pig that he was, he thought she was preferring him to me. And he struck me with his fist, in our quarrel over her. But where is Sawtelle now? I'll tell you, gringo. He is down there in the canyon, riddled with good lead from these faithful guns of mine. And the girl? Ah—she is right here beside me—a poor, weak thing after all and not worth a small part of the trouble she has caused.

"I do not think I will throw her off the trail. After all I have gone through much to hold her. I will keep her—for a while. I think I will start on up the trail now, gringo. But I warn you. Not another foot must you follow. If you do, when you find me I will not have the girl. She will be—down there—on the hungry rocks."

Chuck threw a frantic glance up and back, just in time to see Dex Sublette pull himself from sight over the rounded crest of the rock bulge. Chuck knew relief and a new fear that Alviso would start on before Dex could finish his desperate attack.

Chuck began to talk again and he hardly knew his

own voice, so thin and dry and strained it was. "That which you could have, for the return of the girl, would make you a rich man, Don Diego. You could take it into Mexico with you and it would make you a great man, down there. You could lead an army with it. You might even rule Mexico with it."

Alviso's laugh held the same harsh taunt. "Your promises will not hold me—for I trust no gringo. I have but one regret. I would like to have seen Sublette die. I would like to have been the one who made him die. If I thought that the lead in him was thrown from these guns of mine—ah—then indeed would I be happy. But your promises mean nothing to me, Gringo. I shall keep the girl. And if you follow, you know the answer."

Up on top of the rock bulge, Dex Sublette was trying to find himself, to drive himself back to something near normal, after that ghastly effort which had carried him up to where he was. He could not have told how he had reached there. It seemed that he had had nothing to cling to—yet there must have been something. His fingers and arms felt dead and useless, as though all life had been driven from them by the sustained, terrific effort. The fingers felt wet and clammy and Dex knew that it was blood, running from the torn and crushed flesh.

As though from a distance he heard the voices of Chuck and Alviso, but he made little of them until he caught the words from Alviso. "I shall keep the girl. And if you follow—"

Dex drove himself to his knees and whipped the

mists from his eyes. He peered down into that pocket of blackness below. The starlight reached only part way down, it seemed. But then he caught a stir of movement and that movement resolved itself into an indistinct figure, standing upright and alone. The arms of that figure were raised, as though being flexed for further effort. The head was thrown back and a taunting laugh sounded. And Dex caught the gleam of white teeth. That figure was Alviso!

Without another thought, Dex threw himself out and down. He seemed to fall for ages through space, though the distance was not over a score of feet. The thought came to him, like a flash of fire through his brain, that if he missed, he would go off the trail and on into the eternal depths.

But he did not miss. Full on to the shoulders of Alviso he struck, with an impact which bruised and twisted him with white hot agony. Alviso, flattened to the trail, was for a moment limp, then seemed to rebound like a steel spring. He threw Dex aside and for a moment they both floundered, dazed and half stunned. They struggled upright together. Alviso, snarling like a jungle cat, whipped hands to his guns. And Dex, reaching far, threw all his strength into a mighty blow.

The punch landed on the side of the Spaniard's head. It hurled him sideways, turned him half over in the air—and he dropped beyond the edge of the trail!

Dex stared stupidly at where the Spaniard had been—and was no longer. But up out of the depths, fading like the wail of a fleeting wind, came a long, shrill scream, a scream that rang out and faded swiftly into nothingness. Had sharper ears than Dex's been listening, they would have heard, rising in muffled echo, the thud of something, far below. The hungry rocks had feasted.

Dex dropped to his knees and flattened out slowly on the trail. Something had given way inside him. His brain was whirling, his body washed with weakness. He tried to fight back the blackness creeping over him, but it would not be driven back. It mastered him and pulled him down. . . .

Someone was shaking him back to consciousness. It was Chuck, and Chuck was crying like a baby. "Dex! Dex—we win! Sonia is here—and safe. Dex—you did it. That last long chance you took. Gawd—man—I—I—damn it—I'm blubbering like a kid. The strain—I went through hell. But Dex—we win—we win!"

Dex got slowly to his feet. Somehow he didn't feel alive—and yet he must be alive. For there was Chuck, good old Chuck, holding him and shaking him—and crying.

"Sonia?" croaked Dex.

"She's here. She spoke to me a minute ago, when I cut her loose from her bonds. But she'd been hurt, Dex. Alviso hit her with his fist. She's kind of gone under again. But she'll be all right—all right."

"Where is she?"

Chuck led him to the slim, crumpled little bundle. Dex sat down beside her, lifted her into his arms as

228

though she were a child and rocked her gently and crooned over her.

Later Chuck brought him his boots and chaps and Dex laid Sonia gently down while he donned them. Then he stood up and lifted the girl in his arms. "You'll have to help me, around a piece of this trail, Chuck," he said. "Then I can carry her alone, alone."

Slowly they worked down out of the star-glow and into the blackness of the canyon once more. And Dex moved steadily on with his burden, though that queer, dry lifeless feeling still held him. He couldn't understand that feeling. Though Sonia was in his arms, she seemed a tremendous distance from him. It was as though he was a spirit instead of a mortal man, striding along at his own shoulder. Something had snapped in him—back there when he knew at last that Alviso was done for. And with that breaking tautness, his senses seemed to have failed to function. His moves were purely mechanical. His eyes, sunken far back in a face drawn and lined and set, were leaden and dull. Yet he carried Sonia all the way back to the flat where the outlaw camp had been and where brave men had fought and died.

Chuck went ahead, shouting. A roar of voices came back and men rushed up, crowding around Dex and his burden. Dex did not speak to answer the feverish questions thrown at him. He marched straight along. The flare of the burning buildings had long since gone, but another fire had been built in the middle of the flat, and wounded men lay in blankets about it.

There, beside the flames, Dex halted. With infinite tenderness he laid his burden on the ground. He straightened up, looked once around the circle of wondering eyes, then flattened out on the earth himself, gave a strange, shuddering sigh and was still.

XVII

"I don't know what to make of him. It gives you a queer feeling—kind of like he was here—and yet not here."

It was Wasatch Lane who was speaking, propped up in his own bunk in the Pinon Ranch bunkhouse. His audience was Shorty Bartle, Bill Kirkle and Slim Edwards. It was a week since the great battle in the canyon. These were the wounded. The dead were sleeping, far back down there in the mists of the Thunder River Canyon. "Maybe it sounds queer to you boys," nodded Slim Edwards—"but I've seen the same look about a horse that had broke its heart, running. Old Dex shore is queer."

"He musta gone through hell," put in Bill Kirkle. "Chuck was telling me about that climb Dex made, getting into a position where he could jump on Alviso. Chuck said he had ice water in his veins and that he wakes up now, cold and shaking, dreaming of Dex hanging to that sheer rock, with nothing under him but the canyon. Chuck says he thinks that climb did something to Dex. Maybe he did break his heart, going over that rock."

"There's something wrong," growled Wasatch. "And it's got me worried."

"If I live a million years I'll never get over the disappointment of missing out on that fight," said Shorty weakly. "In this country they'll date time from that brawl."

Shorty was thin and peaked about the face, but his eyes were clear and he was coming along.

"If you're like me," said Wasatch—"you'd want to forget that night—and know you'd never be able to. A lot of good men died—down there. Chick Corcoran, Ben Rellis, Salty Simmons, that strange, curly headed kid who volunteered to ride with our boys. Sometimes I think that it's the memory of those boys that's riding Dex so hard."

"He oughtn't to let it get him down," said Bill Kirkle sagely. "Life's like that. We all knew we weren't riding to any picnic. But life shoves duties in front of every man, now and then, and you jest can't side-step 'em and still keep your own self respect. All the boys who went down there, would be the first to go again, under the same circumstances. So Dex don't want to feel that way too much. Shore we'll miss the fellers who got it. But remembering them will make better men of us."

Wasatch nodded. "You put it pretty well, Bill."

"Me," said Slim—"I'm taking my hat off to Miss Sonia. She shore has got the thoroughbred strain in her. That girl must have gone through hell, cooped up down there with those damned outlaw whelps on all sides of her. And then that damned rat of an Alviso, hitting her with his fist. Why, when Dex brought her up and laid her down beside the fire and the boys saw one side of her face all bruised and swollen—well, they were plenty savage. Yet, the next day when we came up out of the canyon, she rode a horse over that God-awful trail and never blinked. She's the pure quill, she is."

Beyond the limits of the bunkhouse, work was once more in progress about the Pinon Ranch. Until Wasatch and Shorty would be able to be up and around, Joe Edwards and Jumbo Dell were helping Dex and Dolf and Chuck. Milly Duquesne was still staying on, helping Marcia to care for the wounded men. At Milly's request, her father, Jack Duquesne, had rounded up a gruff, but kindly old fellow, Pappy Johns, to do the ranch cooking and Pappy lost no time in losing his heart to Sonia and settling into his little groove in the workings of the ranch.

But Milly was worried about Dex. At first she had been also worried about Sonia, but Sonia was slowly but surely stepping out of the shadows of a dreadful experience. Hidden in her slim body was a spring of endurance and resilience that was amazing. Sonia was drawing away from the past and facing the future with a new found vision and courage.

On the other hand, Milly did not know what to do about Dex. She had the feeling that she didn't know him any more. He was quiet and restrained. He never smiled. He spoke only when he had to. There were deep cut lines about his mouth and there was a set tautness about his face that never left it.

Came a day when Jack Duquesne rode out to the ranch and with him was a sturdy, broad-shouldered, well set up young chap with a ready smile and clear, direct eyes. Milly heard the sound of approaching hoofs and came out on the porch. She looked once, then gave a queer, sobbing cry and raced down the steps. The young fellow was off his horse and opened his arms to her. Milly kissed him and clung to him, laughing and crying.

Dex viewed the arrival from down by the corrals and came stalking slowly up. He wrung the young fellow's hand warmly.

"Hello, Tom," he greeted. "It's good to see you again. This means a lot to me—for Milly's sake."

Tommy Quillian laughed happily. "Means plenty to me too, Dex. I been one lonely son-of-a-gun, what I mean. I suppose you've kept life interesting for Milly—fighting."

Dex shook a grave head. "Not any more, Tom. I—don't know what we'd have done, without Milly. Whenever any of us boys think of all that is kind and loyal and happy, we'll think of Milly. You're going to marry a wonderful girl, Tom. And I want you to remember this. If ever Milly is in need of any help at any time, or anywhere—send word to the Pinon Ranch. We'll ride—to the man."

Milly wasn't laughing any more—but she was still crying. She turned toward the house, pulling Tom with her. "C—come on, Tom darling," she quavered. "I—I want you to meet a wonderful girl—Sonia Stephens."

Inside the doorway, Milly crept into Tom Quillian's arms again and had her cry out. Then, the old brave smile flashing through her tears, she led him into the big living room, where a slim, black haired girl sat beside an open window.

"Sonia," said Milly. "This is Tommy Quillian. We're to be married—shortly."

Sonia stood up and her deep, mystic eyes warmed and glowed. "I am very happy, for both of you. Mr. Quillian, you are luckier than you know. Nowhere, in all the world, is there another like Milly. Knowing her—and loving her—has made me humble—and rich."

Milly had gotten her old flair back. "Here I've been waiting and eating my heart out, for months," she cried. "And now that this wandering man of mine is here, I've got to desert him for a time. Sonia, will you entertain him for an hour. I'm going riding with another man. I'm going to say goodbye to a big brother of mine."

Milly darted out. Sonia smiled gravely at the bewildered Quillian. "In her happiness she would work for the happiness of others. Sit down, Mr. Quillian. She is a very wise, and very generous girl."

Milly found Dex and her father talking together. "Go peddle your papers, Dad," she cried. "Go into the bunkhouse and swap lies with Wasatch and the rest of the boys. Dex is taking me riding."

"You," drawled Jack Duquesne fondly—"are the

234

most shameless young hussy I know. Here your future husband has just showed up after months of absence and you go riding with another man. I don't savvy that."

Milly tossed her red gold head. "You wouldn't. And if I can wait months for Tommy, he can wait an hour for me. Come on, Dex old boy—don't stand there like a dodo bird. Saddle a couple of skates."

They rode out through a westering sun. Dex's face was set in still, grave lines. From the corner of her eye, Milly watched him.

"You want me to be happy, don't you, old timer?" she asked.

Dex nodded. "More, I think, than anything else in the world, Milly."

"No," exclaimed the red-head—"That isn't the proper answer. Not more than anything else. Perhaps next to something else. But not more. Dex—I can't be happy—if I leave you like this. Dex—what is the matter with you? There is something gone out of you. What is it?"

Dex's eyes narrowed. "I don't know, Milly. I'm all dead—in here." He touched the faded shirt over his heart. "I—I can't get away from thinking—thinking."

"Thinking of what?"

Dex's face seemed to harden, his eyes sink under his frowning brows. "Of Chick Corcoran and Ben Rellis—of a curly headed kid who didn't know me from Adam—nor any of the rest of us, for that matter. But he rode into Thunder River Canyon—to die. And

Salty Simmons—good old Salt—who came creeping out of the night, torn with agony, dying—but to tell me where Alviso had gone—with Sonia. He died at my feet, Salt did—for an ideal. You—you can't see men like that die, Milly—without having something die in you, also."

"Stop and think what they died for, Dex," Milly said very softly—blinking her blue eyes rapidly. "As you say, Salty died for an ideal—an ideal that he couldn't live, but which you can. You've got to keep faith with his sacrifice, Dex."

"But why couldn't it have been me—instead of them?" cried Dex savagely, his throat thick and working. "Why couldn't I have died and they have lived?"

"Why question the working of an inscrutable Providence, Dex? What has been, will always be. That trail has been ridden out. And if those men were not afraid to die—then surely you are not afraid—to live."

For a time there was silence between them. Then Dex spoke, very softly. "I had not thought of it—that way. Not to be afraid—to live. That is it, Milly—that is it. Not to be afraid—to live."

His head lifted. His eyes were shining again and the set lines about his mouth softened. He leaned over and laid his hand on Milly's. "Your wisdom, Carrots—is only exceeded by the size of your golden heart. No wonder the fire of the sun is in your hair. For you bring brightness and warmth just like that sun."

"Bu—bu—bosh!" quavered Milly. "All you darned

236

people do—around here—is make me cry. I—I'm going straight back to the ranch, grab Tommy and take him off to marry me. I—I'm through nursing a bunch of knot-headed cow-nurses."

Yet, before they had gone very far, Milly had blinked the mist from her eyes and she was singing softly to herself. For there was a new light in the eyes of the man who rode beside her and a new eagerness in his face.

It was strange, she mused, how she could love Tommy so terrifically—and yet love Dex, also. And how wide apart those two emotions were. For Tommy represented the warm comfort and shelter of a home— a significant symbol of peace and contentment. Tommy's arms would be a strong and comforting haven when the storm winds would rage.

Yet she would think of Dex, for he would be the wild, free spirit of those storms. She would always see him, looming against the far, fierce horizons, purveyor of the romance and color of this tawny, drowsing land.

When she was back in the ranchhouse, Milly went over and hugged Tommy fiercely. "I'll always make you happy, Tommy darling," she whispered.

And then she went to Sonia, tipped her dark head back and kissed her. "Dex has come back, honey," she told her. "The old, smiling Dex is back. He will come to you."

The morning sun lay over the land, building up its layers of shimmering warmth. Yet, down along

Concho Creek, where the aspens and the cottonwoods built blocks of shade, dew still winked on the grass.

Dex Sublette walked slowly up the slope to the ranchhouse, leading two saddled horses. As he turned from the horses he saw her in the doorway. She was as she had been the morning of their first ride together—that morning which seemed incredibly far away. She was slim and vibrant and lovely, her dark head bare, her elfin lower lip soft and red and pure.

"I've been waiting for you," she said.

Dex lifted her into the saddle, swung astride himself, and reined away. They cantered down past the corrals and along the meadows of the creek. They crossed the tumbling waters and went on until the world tipped away from under them and ran down into the shimmering mists which shrouded the canyon of the Thunder River.

Here they dismounted and stood side by side and their eyes ranged far, reaching down that great sage slope to dwell on thoughts that sobered them and held them silent.

"This land," said Dex gravely—"has treated you cruelly. If you hated it forever, I could not blame you."

She shook her head. "I do not hate it. I think, I understand it now. It has tempered me—has made me strong. It has made me see clearly—and wisely. It has taught me that there can be majesty in death and duty in life. It has made me want to welcome that duty. This is my land now. It belongs to me—I belong to it."

Far out there the Thunderheads were strong and

eternal. They seemed to hover and brood in protective-
ness over those wild depths where brave men were
sleeping through the march of all the ages.

A small, hesitant hand crept into Dex's grasp. His
fingers tightened about it. He looked down at the black
head so close to his shoulder, and waited.

Sonia's thoughts were glancing swiftly over the
years. How vaguely distant the past had become! How
remorselessly sure the march of the days and the
months. The world went on and men and women could
cling to it for only a little time.

She looked up at him and met his glance. "I love you,
Dexter Sublette," she said simply.

In the cradle of his arms she rested. The distant cloud
of sage waved and shimmered before the slow push of
the wind. But for these two, the world stood still and
time stood still and even the gossamer gold of the sunlight seemed hesitant. . . .